THE
MIDDLE
SISTER

THE
MIDDLE
SISER

a novel

Bonnie J. Glover

ONE WORLD
BALLANTINE BOOKS • NEW YORK

A One World Books Trade Paperback Original

Copyright © 2005 by Bonnie J. Glover

All rights reserved.

Published in the United States by One World Books, an imprint of The Random House Publishing Group, a division of Random House, Inc., New York.

ONE WORLD is a registered trademark and the One World colophon is a trademark of Random House, Inc.

Library of Congress Cataloging-in-Publication Data can be obtained from the publisher upon request.

ISBN 0-345-48090-2

Printed in the United States of America

www.oneworldbooks.net

2   4   6   8   9   7   5   3

Text design by Susan Turner

Were it not for my mother, Dorothy Marie James, and my father, Lonnie James Jr., both avid readers, this book would not have been written, and I would never have imagined myself beyond the parameters of East New York.

The most important thing a father can do for his children is to love their mother.

—THEODORE HESBURGH

ACKNOWLEDGMENTS

This has been a long journey of discovery and I have many to thank, most especially my friend Eugene Datta, who is unselfish beyond measure. In addition, I'd like to thank Elizabeth Sheinkman, my agent, and Elisabeth Dyssegaard and Melody Guy, my editors, who took a chance on an unknown quantity—me. I hope I live up to their high expectations.

Readers are important, so I'd like to thank my readers, Dr. Rick Bollinger, Kathleen Freeble, Barb Kuroff, Sue Meyer, and Gayle Sipes. Their words of encouragement kept me going, kept me writing when all I wanted to do was go to sleep! They are wonderful!

And of course I had a steady diet of woman power from my friends. Thanks to all who offered words of encouragement and helped when I couldn't get the right word or phrase.

Finally, but certainly not least, my family. My husband, who kept telling me that if this writing thing was easy, everyone would be doing it; my children, Matt and Ben, who smiled and hugged and kissed me even as I fussed a blue streak; and my in-laws, Paul and Valerie Glover, who have acted as surrogate parents over the years. Thanks for all your love. Thanks for all your understanding.

THE
MIDDLE
SISTER

PROLOGUE

BEFORE KWAI CHANG, THERE WAS KATO FROM *THE GREEN HORnet.* On Friday nights we'd sit in front of the television and hum along with the music and play-fight when Kato tore some villain up. The Green Hornet stood around, punched a little, and used a gun. He wasn't even as good as Batman in my book.

Of course, I was alone in loving Kato in my house.

"Please, girl, Kato couldn't do nuthin' 'bout Superman. All Superman gotta do is blow his breath and Kato's butt be back in China." That was mean Theresa, my big sister.

"Huh. Thas just 'cause Superman got some stank breath."

"He do not."

"Yes he do. Just ask anybody that got blowed with it."

"Yeah. Jus' ask anybody." Baby Nona always took up for me, and now she stuck her tongue out at Theresa and stood with her hands on her hips, not hiding behind me or anything.

Daddy poked his head into the room.

"Y'all hush up the fightin'."

And of course we did. Theresa just rolled her eyes and pinched me as I strolled by her, but that didn't mean we were fighting. Just acting the way we normally did, using quiet hollers as we got our punches and last licks in.

But Kato faded from my mind as I grew older and started to read more than I watched television. We had shows we liked, but it was hard with one television and the five of us. Mama loved *Jeopardy* and *Dark Shadows* and any Jerry Lewis movie and would swat at us if we got in her line of vision while her shows were on. Daddy, when he was home, preferred the westerns and shoot-'em-ups on Channel 11.

ONE NIGHT IN FEBRUARY, THERESA CALLED ME FROM THE living room. I was curled up with *Little Women,* crying because I knew Beth was about to die. I was mad with her, mad with the book, and really pissed at Louisa May Alcott. She could have killed Amy. After all, who the hell liked Amy? Even Meg could have gone as far as I was concerned. Losing Beth was bad, really bad. So when Theresa kept on calling, I finally slammed the book shut and headed for the living room.

Before I took two steps out of my room I smelled burnt popcorn and knew somebody had made Jiffy Pop. That was what we ate when we watched movies.

We had a comfortable brown sofa against wood paneling and a throw rug in the middle of the floor that we girls used to lie on to see the TV up close. The black box was in the center of the room, on a stand in front of the radiator. We always had to be careful in the winter not to have the TV too close because sometimes the steam came out fast and squirted hot water. We thought the TV might blow up, but there was no other wall socket to plug it into that the cord would reach.

On the wall behind the TV and between our windows were three pictures. On top was Jesus Christ with a bent head and hands that were reaching out as if he was trying to stroke a child or comfort someone. To his right was Martin Luther King Jr., and President John F. Kennedy was on the left. We had a built-in bookcase beneath that where we kept our *Encyclopaedia Bri-*

tannica and Stories from the Bible that Mama had ordered to make sure we learned about Jesus since we didn't go to church as much as she wanted us to go.

Tonight Mama and Daddy took up the sofa. They shared a tin pan of popcorn. The table lamps were out. The only light in the room was from the television. My sisters had the other pan between them. I sat down and grabbed a handful.

"Look, Pammy, you gotta see this movie." Mama was the only one who called me Pammy. "He remind me a little of that Kato you used to love in *The Green Hornet.*"

I came in on a fight part, where the man, Kwai Chang Caine, was hurling his body through the air and men were falling and running or trying to arm themselves, only to find weapons useless. As I sat with my sisters, with my parents, it was as though I lost all sense of anything else except the man on the screen. I'd never seen anyone more beautiful. Not even Michael Jackson, who was going to be my husband someday.

Even during the commercials I stayed put, willing my bladder to hold on, not wanting to move, afraid to breathe. Daddy talked, saying something about having eaten frog legs when he was in Korea. But for the first time I wasn't interested in hearing his stories. All I wanted to see was the graceful man, the one who held himself tall and spoke so softly that I had to strain to hear. And then the fighting, so like Kato but so different, the slow motion making it seem like dance moves, like a male dancer with bare feet in the sand. He was Kwai Chang, my new hero.

When it was over, I couldn't look at any of them. There had been beauty before me; now, with the lights on again, I saw truth, and it was hard for me to take that he was not real. I almost ran to my room.

When I was settled for the night, I closed my eyes and saw him, saw the curve of his eyes, the strength of his jaw. I sighed.

Watching *Kung Fu* got to be a habit with everyone except Daddy, who was hardly home in the evenings because he worked the night shift and sometimes stayed to work a double. Mama worked too, but not as long as Daddy, and she didn't leave until we were already in school.

WE CAME HOME ONE DAY TO A PILE OF CLOTHES IN THE MIDDLE of the floor and our mother bent with tears.

"Get your things. We gonna leave this place. We gonna leave your Daddy."

Me and Nona looked at Theresa.

"Where the suitcases, Mama?"

"Go look in the closet in my room." She had stood up by then and was wiping at her face, holding a hand over her eye.

"Mama, what done happened to your eye?" It was Nona asking. She was the only one who didn't know.

"Nothing, girl. Just hit it on the door, that's all. Now get them suitcases." Nona and I ran to the back and pulled the hard blue suitcases up front. It took us a small while, dragging the suitcases, bumping them against our knees, stopping to catch our breath. By the time we got back, our old mother was standing where the crying one had been.

"We ain't going nowhere. Y'all help me put these clothes away."

"But Mama, we want to leave," Theresa said. "We don't wanna stay with Daddy no more." I wanted to hit Theresa or at least tell her to speak for herself.

"I'm staying in my house. I got three children and I ain't running away. Besides, we sure ain't got no place to go."

We were quiet that night as we watched *Kung Fu*. We didn't reenact the snatching of the pebble or call each other "grasshopper." I did not try my rice paper moves. Mama sat with us but held her hand on her face, and I was angry with her for reminding me that Daddy hit her.

IN MY BED, I SHUT MY EYES TIGHTLY AND WISHED HARD FOR THE bad feeling to go away, for my mama not to make such a big deal over being hit. He took the belt to us, didn't he? We couldn't go around with a sorrowful face after we got spanked or we'd be spanked again. I went back and forth over our troubles, but it didn't seem like anything made me feel better.

"Why are you sad, little sister?"

My room was dark, the window only a fraction of an inch open, a metal bar propped against it to prevent anyone from getting in. The voice was as gentle as the soft hiss of wind that gathered and swept through the tiny opening.

I opened one eye and then the other. I should have been frightened. I had always been afraid of the dark. And now a voice was speaking to me, and there was only the streetlight a house away playing with the shadows on my wall to keep my room from being pitch black.

I reached for the lamp and blinked a few times after I pulled the chain.

He was sitting on the floor beside my bed, his head cocked to one side as if listening to something far away. His eyes mirrored my fright, and I saw in a glance that if I showed any fear, he would be afraid too and leave.

My heart was pounding, but I slid the covers off me and stood. He uncrossed his legs and rose.

"Forgive me, little sister. I did not want to frighten you by standing at your bed."

I bowed deeply.

"It is an honor, Kwai Chang Caine."

He bowed also and smiled, a shy, lonesome smile that let me know how pleased he was to be with me. And I felt my heart lift. *Kwai Chang and me,* I thought, *a combination, a duo like Batman and Robin, like . . .* I reached for other pairs, but no one else came to mind. *Like no other two,* I said to myself.

"Like no other two," he said, reading my thoughts. "Now tell me of your sorrows, little sister. I am here to listen."

ONE

MY MOTHER DIVORCED MY FATHER BECAUSE HE NAILED DOWN rugs. We ran back to the house when we heard hammering. Breathless, we stood in the doorway and watched. There were small nails at the corner of his mouth, and his forehead was beaded with sweat. His hands could easily have held two hammers, the span wide and the fingers full and blunt.

"Why are you doing that, Daddy?" I asked. Without looking up, he spat the last nail from his mouth and started to hammer, employing short, staccato taps.

"Y'all run in and out of this house all day long and mess up everything. This rug is gonna stay straight."

Mama was at the other end of the room, hands on her hips. Her lips were in a pucker and her eyebrows were so tightly knit they seemed one long, furry caterpillar across her brow. I knew she was angry, but I thought that my daddy was a genius. He had solved the problem of rugs that moved.

Her voice started as a low hum, incomprehensible words tumbling from her mouth, fast and violent, like the dangerous buzzing of honeybees. I don't know what she said as she moved across the room, but the tone of her words hurt me and I flinched, my shoulders hunched near my ears. She stopped in front of him as he continued to hammer, and I felt it a sacrilege for her to be so close to him and so angry. I held my breath. She bent lower and spat the words at him as he had spat the nails from his lips.

"Get out," she said. It came from her depths, a voice she had never used before, forceful and scary. "Get out. I ain't raising my children to be afraid to move. They already afraid to talk."

He looked up, head slightly tilted, hands still clutching the silver-headed tool. There was a moment when I thought he might swing it so that the head would land in the middle of her eyebrows like a miniature moon. But he didn't. He bent and thundered the hammer, the hits more pronounced with each wide, arcing swing. My mother stepped back, fingers over her mouth. She was trembling.

Turning, I ran, hitting one of my sisters on the arm and snatching a hat from the other. *We have to leave,* I remember thinking, *because I don't want to see what will come next.* Theresa and Nona followed with thumping footsteps, slamming the screen door, all of us forgetting the rules against noise and my lessons from Kwai Chang.

After he left, she went crazy, dancing like a holy roller on First Sundays, slipping her clothes off whenever she wanted to feel a breeze between her meaty thighs and watching *Jeopardy* so hard that we didn't see her blink for the entire show. One day we crept on the floor beneath her and raised an old flyswatter with a mirror taped on it so that we could see if she was still breathing. We waited for the puff of air to frost the mirror but instead got a balled fist in our direction and cursed out for bothering her during a Daily Double. We tripped over each other, laughing and running.

We were three girls, Theresa, Nona, and myself, Pamela. And while Daddy lived with us we dragged through the house, cautioned at every footfall that he wanted quiet. We did the best we could, taking care not to giggle loudly or argue with the same voices we used in the streets. But it was hard, moving without sound and speaking in whispers.

I attended P.S. 158 on the corner of Ashford Street and Belmont Avenue in East New York. It was an old school with wide hallways and no lunchroom because children were supposed to go home for lunch or bring it if their parents worked. Mama made us peanut butter and jelly sandwiches and sometimes bread with butter. We kept old jelly jars with the lids so that we could bring drinks; most of the time it was orange juice, but if we didn't have it, water was good enough to drink. Mama said it quenched the thirst just as well and washed the peanut butter down better. I didn't think she was right, but I knew better than to say so. On the water days, I slid my jar in the brown paper bag and kissed Mama with the same type of kiss I always gave her. Nona would wait until we got outside and away from Mama. She would take out the jar, unscrew the cap, and pour the water on the sidewalk.

"I can get piss water from the fountain."

Theresa was only a grade ahead of me at school even though she was two years older. I had been skipped a grade on account of the fact that I could read almost anything by the time I was three. Nona was two grades behind me and smart too but not smart enough to be skipped like me.

In school, I was not good with noise—a chair scraped across the floor, the clicking glide of chalk on the board, or the loud thud of a door slamming made me jump. I found I could only concentrate by sitting still, with my lips closed and my hands folded. I wished all of the children were like me, but I could not control them, and neither could the teacher. School was the exact opposite of home, loud and out of control.

When it was my turn to recite, I programmed myself to move without sound. First I picked my chair up and placed it on the floor so there would be no noise. Then I stood straight with my book in my hands, turning the pages gently so that only I could hear the whisper of air between the leaves. The teacher always praised me for the way I read, and that was enough to make sure I did it the same way all the time.

Mama appeared in every corner of our house, a crooked smile and her finger on her lips, reminding us that Daddy needed his rest, that he had worked an extra shift. She was different in those days—neat and thinner, wearing panty hose without ladders, rushing home from her job as a nurse to cook dinner, sometimes with her uniform still on. She'd look us in the eye, pleading, and wouldn't let us go until she had an answering nod that we would be good and not make noise. When we forgot and tumbled on the floor, pushing and pulling hair, tickling and screeching, I saw a shade of a smile even though she rushed to separate us and make us behave like we had some sense before he yelled from their bedroom.

I practiced quietness with the actor David Carradine, who played Kwai Chang Caine on the television show *Kung Fu*. Kwai Chang walked on rice paper without leaving an imprint. He was my hero. Because of him, I learned every squeaking floorboard and step in the house, placing my feet squarely in the middle or at an angle, avoiding sound as a condition of my apprenticeship with Kwai Chang and my continued survival at home.

I moved with a grace that I tried to instill in my sisters. But they laughed and raised their open palms, using swift chopping gestures, emulating Kwai Chang as he was forced to use violence—which happened in each episode. They did not admire the moves that left rice paper unmolested; their joy rested in the destruction he wrought with a single turn of his wrist or kick from his unshod feet.

"Ah, now look, he need to beat that man's tail. Callin' him yellow. That's just as bad as calling us niggers," my baby sister, Nona, shouted as she moved to the twelve-inch black and white television that sat on a Bassett table acquired from the back of a broken-down truck. Her brown and white cowgirl boots with the silver spurs stomped the floor.

"Girl, what's wrong with you?"

Daddy appeared suddenly, his black belt wrapped around his neck. We knew he was speaking to Nona, but we all muttered, "Nothing," staring at the belt that appeared to grow wider as he brought it from his neck, looping the ends together. He pointed to the wall. We lined up and he gave us each three hard licks on our bottoms. He believed in punishing us all for the sins of one.

His punishment was different from the ones meted out by our mother. Hers were labored beatings that did not hurt us physically. It was mayhem when she spanked us. She cried and we cried.

Whop, whop, whop. He ended with Nona.

"I told you all about the noise. If you wanna watch this show, you'd better sit down and be quiet."

On television, Kwai Chang ducked his head, trying not to fight. When Daddy left, we sat and finished watching, not crying although our backsides burned. I sighed at the fading picture of the Chinaman in silhouette, a searcher, walking in the sand alone.

ON THE DAY MY FATHER LEFT, BEFORE I KNEW HE WAS GONE, I was in bed listening to the sounds of the house, little creaking noises that he'd once explained were the sounds of the house settling.

"A house can take as long as it wants to hunker down and get comfortable. That's about all it does. Tries to get just right for the family that's in it."

My head had been against his heavy chest as he explained about houses and why I shouldn't be afraid because he was there. He had pushed my bangs out of my eyes with his large blunt fingers and smiled slightly, teasing me about being concerned.

"Funny child." He'd cuffed me on the chin and put me down. I was lost when we were not touching. I breathed in his musky smell and moved closer, but he swung his legs from the bed and started to walk off.

"Where you going, Daddy?"

"Going to see the turtle make water." He'd slid away from me and out of sight.

The evening he left, our mother met us downstairs with minute pieces of Kleenex stuck to her face and eyes that darted back and forth quickly between the three of us, never stopping or resting on any one daughter. We stood together as she explained, but we already knew. He had stopped by the foot of my bed the night before, but I pretended not to hear him. Then he went to Nona and finally to Theresa. But no one moved, no one breathed as he said good-bye. There was silent communication between the three of us, and we each pretended to be dead.

"I gotta go," he said to me. "I'm sorry 'bout all of this, but I can't stay being the way I am and she can't let me stay bein' the way she is." There was a shuffle, then quietness. Then pain in my middle because I had not said good-bye.

I pushed deeper into the sheets and thought of my father swinging a hammer. I knew we'd been safe as long as he was around, tap-tapping at the rug, beating the nail into the floor, making things straight, the way they should be. What I didn't know was how things were going to be without him. I'd never lived without the sound of the hammer in the background.

TWO

THEY CAME IN THE MIDDLE OF THE NIGHT, SCRAMBLING OVER us like cockroaches revealed with the glare of naked light or like mice scurrying for cover after a righteous shoe is tossed in their direction. There were three of them, Zora and Aurora, the eldest and twins, as well as Pinky, the baby. They were Mama's sisters come to cry with her, come to help her, come to make her feel better now that Daddy was gone. And, they said, come to put their wild-ass nieces in check.

We thought Auntie Zora, with her horn-rimmed glasses and big pocketbook that she swung at us, was the worst sister. She smelled of cigarettes and Vicks, and her tits were so small Nona and I wondered if she had any at all. Which always led us to another discussion: was there a dick or wasn't there one?

We had to look out for Auntie Aurora too because she was unpredictable evil. That's what Theresa said. One minute she was fussing and you were in a little trouble, but then let a grown-up come up and the whole situation changed. She always needed to show how tough she was. Her voice would become shrill and contentious. Things would go from bad to worse in less time than it took to shake a stick at somebody. Where it started with "Young lady, watch your tone," it became "I see I'ma have to take my shoe off to walk all over that ass."

Pinky was cool. She didn't care for us one way or the other. She was glad to be away from home, taking in the sights of Ashford Street and ignoring children who weren't hers.

Mama said her piece during their first visits, made like clockwork beginning every other Thursday and lasting until late Sunday evening. We didn't see how they could have jobs, coming up from Virginia on the train every week like they did, but when we asked Mama she explained.

"They all got good jobs. Your aunt Zora work for the telephone company. Aurora do something for the county, and Pinky, well, she do some kind of anything. Can't tell too much where her money come from."

"How come they always running up here?"

"They ain't never took no days off. Zora been working at that phone company for ten years and ain't never took no time. Now they using it to come see about us. That's what family do for each other."

We didn't tell Mama that we wished they wouldn't come see about us. Theresa said telling her might make her sadder, but I couldn't think that she wasn't sad enough without them coming and carrying on every weekend. A body couldn't find no peace when they was around.

We'd never seen them so much when Daddy lived with us. He hated them and had told us to make sure we didn't turn out to be "no big bitter women."

"He wouldn't even let them talk. They had to go 'round on tiptoe. I couldn't let 'em live like that. I couldn't. And then he was so mean. Makin' 'em line up to get spanked. Like they was in the army or something. And did I tell you . . ." She leaned over and whispered, but I didn't have to hear her telling that Daddy hit her. Mama couldn't hold no secrets.

"Girl, you know you did the right thing. Can't no man come

between a woman and her childrens. You gonna be all right. Just come on, put God first and I guarantee ya, He gonna see about you and these here big girls you got," Aunt Zora comforted Mama. The pocketbook was at her feet, and she had her hands around Mama's shoulders, rubbing.

Pinky was in the living room having a beer. She had sent me and Theresa to the store earlier for a six-pack and had already downed three. Each time we passed through the room she'd roll her eyes and ask, "What y'all heifers looking at, huh?"

Whenever they stayed over they expected me and Theresa and Nona to wait on them like queens. They got the bedrooms and we slept on the pullout in the living room, two at the head and one at the foot. Every night Nona cussed a blue streak as she hit the flat pillow.

"Why the hell these bitches gotta be here?"

"Mama need 'em right now. She sad about Daddy." Theresa was patient and kept telling Nona the same thing, and Nona kept saying the same thing back to Theresa.

"Why she need them when she got us?"

"Just go on to sleep, Nona. We got school in the morning."

THEY KEPT COMING BACK AND COMING BACK. ALMOST LIKE A movie we saw where the people wouldn't die but just kept getting right back up to do the same thing over and over again. Behind their backs we started calling them the Zombie Sisters, and when we could, when we knew they weren't paying attention or looking in our direction, we'd walk with straight staring eyes and rigid arms right in back of one of them. The bet was to see how long you could follow one without getting swatted. Nona always won because she didn't care if she got hit or not. They'd pop her with a quick backhand and she'd grin and turn around and try it on another aunt as soon as she could.

Things settled into a routine of visitations, and we were finally able to sleep through the night without Mama and her sisters keeping us up with their card parties and laughing and hyena cries. They acted like they were kids again, playing around and insulting each other and talking bad about my daddy. And it was bad when they got drunk. Then they all took turns crying except for Pinky, who couldn't squeeze pee out of her pussy, much less a tear from them evil eyes of hers.

The first time I heard Mama weeping, I crept from my room only to find Theresa and Nona already by the dining room door. We looked in, and it seemed to me as if we were one body, one pair of eyes drinking in the scene in front of us. Mama was on the floor, on her side, twisted and writhing, moving with heat. Tears coursed down her face, and every few seconds a weird moaning sound came from her throat. She was holding her stomach and then she would say, "Oh Lord, oh Lord. I'm in such pain. Take this away from me."

Aurora and Zora were trying to calm her, to hold on to her, but Mama kept sliding away from them like a snake, all slippery and hard to hold. And her sisters were drunk too, unable to stand or even kneel to get her straightened out. Pinky sat at the dining room table, her legs crossed, not saying anything, like she wasn't there and didn't see Mama on the floor crying like she'd lost all her natural mind.

Zora finally got a hold of Mama's arm and was trying to make her get up when she lost her balance and landed on her butt, shaking the floor and making the punch bowl next to the sink shift to the edge. Nona pushed it back before it fell.

In the meantime, Mama moved to the place on the rug where Daddy had last hammered a nail, and she laid her head on the spot, rubbing her cheek back and forth against the carpet. It got so quiet in the room that we heard each other breathe and exhale and breathe again.

And then, of course, Kwai Chang appeared, formless at first but emerging through the haze of their cigarette smoke. He was sitting on the floor next to Mama, cross-legged with his head angled toward her as though in deep meditation. His fingers were settled on his knees, and his face was creased deep with worry. He stood and bowed toward me. I nodded in his direction, careful to make it only a twitch of a bow.

Chang had on his hat, with a bedroll of some sort slung across his shoulders, and of course his feet were bare, long bony toes without a proper home.

"I've waited for you to get here," he said aloud.

"I'm glad to see you, Kwai Chang," I replied.

"I am sorry that I cannot stay. There are too many women here." He nodded at my mother and her sisters and then at me and Nona and Theresa.

I wanted to protest that I needed him to stay.

"You must understand, there is too much that is being said that should not be said and too much that should be voiced that remains unspoken. Time for me to go, Grasshopper, time for me to go."

He bowed from the waist and began to disappear without waiting for my reply. I could only take a deep breath and sigh and wonder why he had shown up in the first place only to leave so quickly. An aunt speaking brought me back to the scene of my mother flooding tears into the carpet, and my heart stopped for a moment, her grief too much for me to see.

"Geneva, you need to stop this shit. Ain't no man worth all what you going through."

It was Pinky. She sat on her chair, staring at Mama. And you could tell that she was disgusted, the way she puffed on her cigarette and shook her head at the same time. She uncrossed her legs slowly.

"I ain't never thought I'd live to see the day when my big sister would go ass-crazy over no nigger. Girl, you need to get yourself together. This ain't no way for your daughters to see you. Hell, I ain't even wanna see no more of this pathetic shit. I'm going to bed."

Pinky stood. She took another puff from her cigarette and put it out. She went to stand by my mother, who had stopped whimpering and was wiping her face with the back of her hand. She bent down by Mama and blew the cigarette smoke in her face.

"Get your act together."

When Pinky left, Theresa, Nona, and I got our mother up and helped her to bed. I bathed her face with a cool washcloth, and Theresa and Nona helped her into nightclothes. Mama didn't say a word, and I remember thinking that her quietness was as scary as her loud wailing. In fact, I preferred the crying because her quietness made me think she'd given up all hope.

In the morning the sisters were gone, leaving a note for Mama and a twenty-dollar bill.

But they came back again.

"You know he wasn't no good, Geneva. He wasn't nuthin' but a dog of a man and he ain't never take care of you the way he should have. He ain't never." Aurora was talking, and when she finished she took the shot glass that had been in the palm of her hand, stirred its contents once with her index finger, and then downed the drink in one gulp. There was a bottle of Jack Daniel's on the table. It was four o'clock in the afternoon.

They were sitting around the kitchen table smoking and drinking when we got home from school. There was a deck of playing cards, coasters, and four ashtrays, one for each sister, overrun with pink-tipped ends sitting amidst the ashes like little anchors.

Pinky had to have her say too.

"Big Sis, your man wasn't shit. You know he was trying to get with me. He wasn't no good."

They had been going around the table, one after another, talking stuff about my daddy. I stood in the doorway, holding my books and my sweater. But I felt sick to my stomach. I wanted to vomit and make sure that I vomited all over each of them. I didn't look behind me, but I knew Theresa and Nona were right there, one on each shoulder.

"Hush up," said Zora, nodding at the doorway and us.

Theresa pushed past me.

"Naw, why you gonna stop talking 'bout our daddy now? Jus' cause we here? Go on, get it all out." She was loud. Anybody who knew Theresa knew she was gonna cry. Mama got up to put a hand on her shoulder, but my sister shook it off.

"You the worst one. Letting 'em sit up in here and say what they wanna about Daddy. You ain't right neither."

Nona stepped up beside Theresa, and her hands were clenched and her teeth touched the bottom of her lip as though she were ready to bite through. But maybe for Nona it was more that she hated the aunts than she loved our father. I went to stand beside my sisters and glared with them at the other women in the room. Then I said to myself that I wouldn't be the kind of sister who'd sit up in my sister's house and hurt either one of them with mean words. I wouldn't do it.

Mama faced her sisters.

"The children right. We ain't got no call to speak bad about they father. No more talking about him. It's finished."

"What you say?" Aunt Aurora got up so fast the chair she was sitting in overturned, one of its spindly wooden legs twisting off. For a moment I thought it breathed a sigh of relief from not having to hold her three-hundred-pound behind anymore. She might not have titties, but her butt more than made up for the loss up top.

"Y'all heard me. Your comments about their daddy ain't welcome. He may be all that you said and more, but he still they daddy and you gotta stop."

That's when Zora jumped up, nostrils flaring and size 48DD's heaving. That was always peculiar to me, them being twins and all but one having no chest and the other being blessed beyond need.

"You gonna talk that way to us, your own sisters, over these . . . these . . . bad-ass girls you got? They can't help you do nuthin'. Nuthin'."

Pinky stood now. I guess she felt left out.

"Girl, I was just telling the truth. Your man was always trying to get in my drawers. You might as well know that." The way she said *man* and made an ugly mouth when it came out told me and everybody else what she thought of my daddy.

"Daddy ain't want none of your stank ass." That was me before I could think not to say anything, and the words were on the table and everybody was standing back and breathing hard.

"Little bitch, how you gonna be talking to me like that? Here, Zora, Aurora, whichever the fuck one you are—take my earrings 'cause I'm bust Miss Prissy one across her mouth."

"You ain't doing nuthin' to my girls." Mama stepped in between my aunt and me and let her eyes work Pinky into falling back. "I think y'all need to pack up and go." Her voice was strong, but her head was turned away from her sisters and toward us. I knew she was sorry for the way they carried on and for letting them come here in the first place. I was jumping up and down inside. The Zombie Sisters were vacating the premises.

Aunt Zora wanted to argue the point some more, but her twin took Pinky's arm and the three of them managed to squeeze past us. Pinky stepped on my toe, hard, and leaned forward to stick out her tongue. She said something like I was lucky she hadn't hurt me. Within an hour they were packed and downstairs, headed for the corner of Sutter and Ashford to hail a cab.

"Don't you be expectin' no help from us. Let your grown-ass kids help you. We ain't coming back and we ain't sendin' y'all nuthin'." That was Auntie Aurora yelling at Mama as they worked to carry their bags down the street.

"Promises, promises," Nona muttered under her breath as

we peeked out the window and watched two barrel-butts and one half-barrel waddle down the block. Mama didn't say anything for the rest of the evening. She sat by the window and lit cigarette after cigarette until the room choked with white smoke.

Later that night, drifting off to sleep in my room, I heard a rustling, and when I turned over, Theresa and Nona were in my room. They fell on my bed, and all of a sudden we were giggling and pinching and punching each other for no reason. Just like the old days before Daddy left.

"Girl, I thought I'd pee my pants when you told that pussy that Daddy wouldn't want her stank ass." Nona sat up, tilted her head to the side, and fixed her mouth the way Pinky did. Theresa fell off the bed holding her stomach.

"I ain't never thought you had it in you—to talk like that to somebody. What happened?" Theresa said this as she climbed on the bed again, trying to catch her breath.

I shrugged, but inside I knew it was all because of my daddy. Because each time they rolled him through the meanness of their hearts right up through their lips, a part of me felt stepped on. It hurt too much to let them talk. And that pain had pushed up from my chest and forced itself out before I knew it. I had said those words, and a part of me was very proud of the fact that I did say them instead of crying in the corner somewhere or swallowing them down. Kwai Chang was right. Things unsaid had to be said.

No one kissed in our family. But before they left, Theresa squeezed my hand and Nona gave me the peace symbol. It was what we could do for each other.

THREE

THE QUIET IN ME WAS AT WAR WITH THE PART OF ME THAT wanted to yell and cry when my daddy left us. I thought of him constantly. I did not think that he could leave us and not come back. I loved him.

Sometimes I sat on the edge of the bed, on his side, and sniffed in the bathroom for the Old Spice we gave him every year for Christmas. I practiced being so quiet that I could sneak up on either my sisters or my mother. I wanted to be invisible. I thought if I grew quieter, neater, cleaner, somehow he would find out and make his way home. Once I tried to talk to Nona.

"You know we was too noisy. He needed to rest an' we was busy runnin' and jumpin' through the house."

She had big eyes and a small round head.

"We wasn't loud. Mama made us be outside. He ain't want us."

"How can you say that? He wanted us. He did."

She shrugged, and I continued to whisper fiercely at her, trying to make her understand.

"It was Mama really. She made him go just because he wanted to fix things up and wanted everything to be nice." I was whisper-screaming now and had moved close to Nona, in her face. I got angrier then because I saw her pity. She made me feel like I was the baby and she was the one who knew about the world even though I was two years older. I turned away from her before she could see me crying.

"Yeah, it could've been Mama. Guess I would get tired of people messin' up the house if I wanted it to be neat."

That was all she said, but it hit me that I had to stop talking about him. No one else did. And when I talked about him I got louder instead of quieter and made everything worse because I was supposed to be quiet.

I went to my room and closed the door. I sat in the middle of the floor and cried without a sound, tears falling down my cheeks, my tongue catching them before they rolled to my chin. It hurt in my throat.

When I finished I wiped my eyes and promised myself it was the last time that I would cry for him. I stood in the center of my room and started to practice my moves, imagining Kwai Chang alongside, the slow, structured ritual soothing my nerves.

First my hands, made limp and then floating above in movements I thought made sense, for I knew nothing of real kung fu, only what I saw in the opening credits and what I imagined to be a true portrayal. Then my feet moved in unison with the ghost searcher who appeared at my side, whisper-light on the carpet, planted with daintiness so as not to leave a dreaded imprint.

Kwai Chang nodded gravely at my movements, obviously impressed that I was able to follow him, shaking his head at my mastery.

"You have progressed well." He said this in the halting speech of one obviously a non-native. I smiled and bowed to him in response. He disappeared, and I sat down and crossed my legs. I meditated and listened to my heartbeat and to the breaths. I cleared my mind of everything except my father, and

I asked God to bring him home or help me forget, whichever He thought was best.

THE FIRST TIME SHE PUT THE MUSIC ON AND MADE US SHUT OFF the television to listen we were surprised. It was Sunday morning. She went through the house and opened up the windows and turned the volume up full blast. She banged on each bedroom door and made us come out into the living room.

Her housecoat was buttoned wrong and her Afro wig abandoned, so we saw the small plaits squared to her head. Her eyes were feverish in the way she gazed over each of us, unfocused yet determined.

"We ain't going to church, but we gonna have some church up in here. You all sit an' listen to 'The Mighty Clouds of Joy.' If you get a notion to dance—go ahead. I'm gonna dance to the Lord today."

We didn't have a notion to dance, but she did, holding her hands in the air as she pranced about our living and dining room, sometimes muttering, "Glory," sometimes screaming, "Jesus Lord," always singing the chorus: "Come on and ride, ride the mighty clouds." As the music reached its highest point her arms flailed wildly and her voice tried to rise along with the Mighty Clouds, but she was left behind because of having no breath and no ability.

We were afraid of what she was doing. Church was for Easter and Thanksgiving weekend and maybe Christmas if it fell on a Sunday. And then we went straight to the staid folds of Daddy's Catholic church, immense and cavernously cold. The priests did not talk of riding the mighty clouds of joy with Jesus. Mama's religion was hot, pulsing, making her gyrate her hips and move to an alien rhythm.

The three of us were on the sofa close together, our legs pressing against one another. My eyes were down because I could not look. So much noise and so much graceless movement made me ashamed. The Chinaman appeared, but his face remained half turned from me, focused also on Mama. He did not know what to make of her antics either. Then he turned his warm brown eyes on me, making them narrow as though he were in some desert storm. And I was even more ashamed that he saw her the way that I saw her, the way that Daddy might have seen her too.

Nona nudged her leg against mine, but I knew before I turned that there was going to be a gleam in her eyes and that she was laughing at Mama, because Nona laughed at everything. I kept my eyes on my lap. In my head I asked Kwai Chang to leave. I told him that it was a private moment between our family and that he was intruding. He melted away.

Theresa, the only one of us with her eyes glued to Mama, got up when the music stopped and went into the kitchen. Mama finally eased herself into the La-Z-Boy after she turned off the stereo. Her forehead was beaded with sweat. She groaned as she sat.

Theresa came back with a glass of ice water and a napkin and waited in front of our mother. Mama took the glass and downed it in one gulp.

I thought by this time there might be some shame, that she might notice the three of us and say that she was sorry for being so crazy and for dancing so wild and so hot when she didn't have to act that way. But there was nothing but tiredness on her face.

When I finally got up enough courage to leave the room, I wondered what Mama would do next.

"Hey, Pam, hey, Pam, hold up."

I stopped and waited for Chuckie to catch up. He was a black-skinned boy whose face reminded me of an old, worn penny. Sometimes I thought I could see what he would look like as an old man, his serious mouth turned down and dimples covered with gray hairs on his cheek. When he smiled at me my heart pounded and climbed in my throat and I pretended to look over his shoulder so that my eyes might not tell my secret.

"You going to class?"

"Yep."

"Well, look, I got something for you."

"What?"

We were in the locker area and the bell rang for third period, three short blasts. There were kids around, some leaning against the walls, some on the floor gathering books from their bottom lockers.

I was standing in front of him and tried not to see his face, but I felt trapped. Before I knew what was happening, he grabbed my shoulders and planted a kiss on my lips. The pressure was hard but his lips were soft, parted so that I caught the tiniest scent of peppermint before he ran away.

"There," he said. "Happy Valentine's Day."

I stood by myself in the yellow hallway and wondered why he'd done what he'd done, and savored the thought of my first kiss.

There was no one to tell, so I kept the kiss a secret. At home I daydreamed more than usual, but Theresa was too full of Mama and helping her that she didn't notice me when I stopped to touch my lips or smile to myself. Nona swished around the house, loud and full of angry laughter. She barely noticed me either.

THE DOOR TO MY BEDROOM WAS SWOLLEN. DESPITE MY TUG-ging and pushing, it was sluggish. And I was happy to do something to stop thinking about Chuckie. I put on my Craftsman apron and found the red toolbox that Daddy had given me for my tenth birthday. I took my time, all the while hearing his voice in my ear full of patience, coaching me through all the steps.

I removed it, standing on a chair to reach the topmost hinge, twisting the blue-handled screwdriver with the tips of my fingers, pausing every so often to take it back in my hands, to feel the heft and weight of it in my palms.

The second hinge was breast high, and it was off in seconds. My fingers worked less cautiously now that the movements were becoming familiar again. My father's voice was a drone in my left ear, and although I caught a glimpse of Kwai Chang, he kept his distance, knowing that it was my time with my daddy.

I was on my knees for the last hinge, my body and free arm bracing against the door to keep it propped up. I had a drop cloth on the side, careful of the floor. I had to move the door onto the cloth, placing it on its side.

Measuring the length of the opening was tricky. I stood on the same chair but finally gave up doing it by myself and screamed for Nona.

"You ain't got to yell, we right here."

All three of them stood behind me, staring.

Nona took the measuring tape to the bottom of the opening and gave me the number. Then she helped me measure the door itself. The other two were silent, and I felt as if I were on some stage and they were my audience, attentive and watching every move that I made. Suddenly Daddy's voice was inadequate and my fingers slippery and untrained. I dropped the pencil and broke the lead that was to mark the door a quarter of an inch shorter. Nona sucked her teeth and went in search of another pencil. I went back to the toolbox, searching to find what I might need to shave the door to size.

Once I relaxed again and forgot that they were staring, it was easy. The trick was to be steady, to have a good eye, and never to let distractions intrude. Work with the grain, never against it. All the advice he'd ever given me was in my ears, and although I was tired and sweat stung my eyes, I kept on until the door was finished.

Nona helped me put it back on its hinges, and Theresa and Mama watched as we had a test run. It opened smoothly into my bedroom now. They clapped, and I grinned. The memory of Chuckie's kiss, my first, swept over me, and I felt like telling them. I looked down at my broken nails and the sawdust on the floor and the moment was gone, even though I felt the cool press of his mouth on mine and smelled his peppermint-spiced breath.

The kiss had been a dream, I decided. My hands, callused and bruised, were the reality, and for some reason I could not bring myself to share more than that real moment with them. It would hurt too much to dance in front of them and be laughed at like Nona had laughed at Mama or to be pitied by Theresa.

FOUR

CHUCKIE AND I STARTED GOING TOGETHER. HE HELD MY HAND for short minutes and greeted me every day at my locker with a quick kiss, and I got used to his sweetness pressing against me. But that was all we had. He never asked for more, and I never gave him anything. But I wanted him, especially when I breathed in his scent and knew that he had sucked a peppermint before touching my mouth.

One day I was angry. I don't know why. Slamming my books into the locker, throwing my coat.

Chuckie waited and then gently took me by the shoulders. But I was not used to gentleness, and I did not want it.

"You know what? Why don't you leave me alone? I don't want you around me anymore. You're like a puppy that won't go home. You go home."

He asked me if I was sure, all the time staring at me with hooded eyes. I thought he might cry. If he had, I was prepared to make fun of him, to ridicule him in front of whoever was in the hall. I was not going to be his girl. It was time to stop it— these stupid kisses every morning, the soft brown eyes wondering over me, holding me hostage with their love.

"Yes. Go."

He turned and left me standing in the overly bright hallway and never spoke another word to me. And I put him out of my mind.

MAMA USED TO SMELL OF AVON. SHE HAD A BOTTLE OF PERfume sitting on her side of the dresser, and it was shaped like a white woman in a long dress with a pointed nose and chin. This woman fascinated me, and I would sit and hold her and examine her skirt and touch her nose that wasn't like mine and wonder what it would feel like to have such a delicate face and hair that flowed instead of catching in the comb. Sometimes I winced in pain as Theresa combed out the knots in my kitchen. The woman bottle didn't have a knotty kitchen. I could tell by her smile there was no place on her head that hurt when it got combed.

But now the woman was neglected and Mama began to smell like the rectangular patch of dirt we had inside the front gate of our house, the dirt neighborhood strays came to pee in and cats knocked our garbage over into. Mama became oily and her hair hung on her neck, full of dandruff. She didn't comb it. And she stopped giving us hugs. Not long ones or short ones. Not ones to comfort and not ones just because we were near and she could catch us and hold on.

We came home from school one day and she was sitting in the same chair we had left her in when we marched out of the door.

Theresa went to stand in front of her.

"Mama, you need a shower."

Mama put a finger to her hair and glanced up at Theresa, surprised.

Theresa nodded. "Yeah, you need to wash your head too. I'll plait it up for you when you get finished."

That's when Mama stood, tightening the belt on her robe and nodding almost without knowing who she was nodding to or what she was nodding about. I know that for a fact because I didn't see anything in her eyes when her head went up and down. Mama was right in front of us, pink robe and all, but there wasn't anyone coming from behind her eyes.

When she moved from the seat, turning to go up the stairs, both Nona and I choked. Theresa, who had moved toward the stairs, waiting for Mama, saw our faces and walked back, taking Mama's hands and pulling her forward with gentleness. I could see Theresa's face. I knew she didn't want to look but she had to. It was about being the oldest and about facing things the way they were and not always thinking about the way they should be or used to be.

The back of Mama's robe was stained with blood, dried and caked, and so was the seat of the chair she had been sitting in all day. Nona was still, and Theresa paused for only a second.

"Y'all put that chair out to the garbage."

And that was that. We obeyed.

From then on, when Mama took to her spells and couldn't seem to focus or understand that we were hers, Theresa took over. Both Nona and I were grateful. We had Theresa, and she counted for a lot when Mama drifted to wherever she went when her eyes refused to stay on us and her body settled unmoving in some place far away.

For months after he was gone, after her sisters left, my mother sat in our living room and sipped tea from a broken cup and ate burnt toast slathered in butter. She stopped going to work, and they stopped calling for her to come in. She never raised her voice, never spoke above a whisper, but insisted that on Sundays we play loud religious music. When neighbors knocked on the door and asked that the music be lowered, she'd nod, clutch her pink hooded bathrobe, and climb the stairs to her bed.

ONE SUNDAY, EARLY IN THE MORNING, WHILE MAMA STILL slept, we went to the stickball park down the street from the house. It wasn't a stickball park for real. Everybody called it that because it was an open field and that's the game we played there most of the time.

I don't know what got into our heads, why we thought we should go and play, but we did and it felt good. We used squashed soda cans for the bases and screamed whenever we connected with the ball. Nona was the best, and when she rounded third base, headed for home, me and Theresa waited to tackle her to the ground and tickle her until she screamed uncle. She had to tell us that we were better and that she was only a lowly flea. We laughed so hard our ribs hurt, and for the first time in months we cried glad tears instead of sad ones that we did not want to share.

Maybe we'd been there for an hour, maybe an hour and a half, when we heard this voice calling us from the side of the street. The little Harris boy from the house next door was panting through the link fence that surrounded the lot.

"My mama sent me to get y'all. She say you better come quick. Your mama done gone crazy in the street." He was breathing hard from having run down the block, but we understood. It was as if we had been waiting, holding our breath even in between the tickling and running, waiting for Mama to do something to bring us back to where we didn't care to be—the present. We didn't look at each other and we didn't glance back at the boy.

Nona tore up the concrete, and Theresa was close behind. I knew I had to rush, but I didn't want to see her. There was a knot in my stomach the size of the pink rubber ball we'd been playing with, and the closer I got to the house, the bigger the knot got. The Harris boy passed me on the side of the street, looking back and waving his hand for me to hurry.

Mama stood in the front yard. The black wrought-iron gate was closed, but the neighbors surrounded the outside of the yard, standing with her but cut off from being too close. They were mostly women and mostly silent, holding on to their children, rocking the babies over their shoulders.

Our mother was dressed from head to foot in white. Her nurse's uniform was buttoned wrong and her panty hose bunched at her ankle, creating a wrinkled, unkempt look. I remembered the commercial on television about the elephant at the zoo and the woman with bagging hose who was embarrassed. But our mother was not embarrassed.

Her nurse's hat tilted to the side, held from falling by her ear. The braids that Theresa had plaited for her stuck straight up from her head. Mama resembled Miz Fanny Harper, a lady on the block who'd lost her mind too.

While Mama stayed in the house most times, Miz Harper walked up and down the street pulling girls' dresses down and telling them not to rub their titties because they got big if you touched them. She went around wearing short, short skirts with white tights and go-go boots. Men pointed and laughed when Miz Harper walked by up and down the street asking for a date, her two stubby teeth perched in the middle of an otherwise empty mouth, lips covered with the pinkest shade of gloss she could find. She always wanted to go uptown to see James Brown at the Apollo. After she stopped a man and asked him out, she'd move in closer to him and do a few steps to show she could dance. The good-natured ones shook it on down with her for a beat or two. My daddy was one of them, rocking back and forth with Miz Harper and then stopping just when she was throwing the moves on him.

"Miz Harper," he'd say, "I can't go it like you. 'Sides, you know my Geneva ain't gonna allow me to go to no Apollo with a fine sister such as yourself. Now get on outta here with them boots. You just a dancin' machine, woman, and you gonna get me in trouble."

"I'se just asting. Ain't no harm in that."

"G'on now, 'fore you get me in trouble."

Miz Harper would head up the street, and Daddy would turn to us grinning.

"That woman shure nuff got some moves." And then he'd laugh. But it wasn't mean laughter. It was just like he couldn't believe a woman near enough to eighty to lick it still wanted to boogie.

I wondered what type of laughter we could expect with Mama, the loud index-finger-pointing laughter or the quieter, I'm-sorry-about-your-situation type. And then I wondered if we could ever forgive her for making this spectacle. My entire mouth was dry by the time I pushed through the crowd to the front.

I had to take a deep breath. *Kwai Chang,* I thought, and before I could finish his name he was behind her, inside the gate, glancing over her shoulder and fixing me with a gentle smile. Somehow the sight of him diminished the ball in my stomach and helped me relax my hands, which were clenched at my side. Whatever new humiliation she would bring to us, I was going to be prepared.

Mama was speaking, and the women on our block were listening. Clasping the family Bible with thick-wristed hands that were strong and did not tremble, Mama rested the book on top of the gate.

"The New Testament, it say that a man must leave his mama and daddy and cleave unto his wife. That ain't happenin' here. My husband done left me. He cleavin' to somebody else."

I felt like laughing, and I thought others might. But there was only a polite cough while Nona dug her elbow into my side and Theresa took a deep, sorrowed breath at my other side.

"If that ain't enough, my own sister came here and let me know that he done tried to get with her." She looked around the crowd, wide-eyed and frightening.

"According to this here Bible—" She raised the book in the

air with some effort, holding it in front of her as though it were a shield. Some women in the audience put their hands on their throats, and some moved back—not so much because of Mama but because of the strength of her holding the book, thinking her full of conviction and speaking the truth instead of crazy out of her mind.

"In the time of Moses, it say a man can divorce his wife if she is fornicating. Well"—and here she turned to us—"I been protecting my girls and they feelings for a long time but today I'ma hafta do something. I'ma divorce this man according to the law Moses done put down."

Mama held the Bible higher and moved from the gate. I saw one neighbor, Mrs. Gibson, reach out and take her daughter's hand; another picked up her son and pressed his ears to her bosom. Nona was rigid. Theresa stepped forward. My mother's voice rang out clear and loud without a tremble.

"I divorce you, Louis Mack Johnson. I divorce you, Louis Mack Johnson. I divorce you, Louis Mack Johnson."

Each time she said it she turned around in a small circle. Instead of the concrete, her feet turned in the rectangle of black dirt that had been a garden in better days, when Daddy lived with us.

Mama was still after the last rotation, staring into the crowd, her eyes peeling away the layers of other women, her daughters, her sisters.

"I ain't saying none of y'all have to do the same thing. Y'all do what you need to. But I gotta live with my daughters. They gotta know that sometimes men can't come back. Sometimes the things done is too wrong. And making it so there is no joy in the house and bringing somebody else's juices into my bed—well, that's too much to take. Too much to stand." She nodded to us then.

"He can still be your daddy. I ain't never gonna stop that.

But he can't be my husband no more. I done give him a bill of divorcement, heard by y'all here."

Mama closed the Bible with a thump. She turned away, back straight and nurse's hat tilted, and climbed the five stairs to our door.

"Girls, it's time for you to come in and get cleaned up. Y'all look like shit."

Kwai Chang tilted his head as we followed Mama up the stairs.

"She is a brave woman," he said.

FIVE

It took a year, but it was a relief when we lost the house, because things were falling apart. Water leaked through the roof and onto the floors. The tiles near the bathroom sink buckled, and the paint, inside and out, chipped and tore away from the walls. At night I'd find a different bare patch and I'd run my fingers over it, trying to smooth the roughness, consoling the house because of our missing father.

The day we moved, Theresa handled Mama and Nona handled the movers, directing them with a hard-edged, sour voice that seemed strange coming from a thirteen-year-old. But she had to be tough. They weren't real movers, just guys from down the street who needed the ten dollars Mama promised. Nona cussed so long and so hard at one man because he dropped a box of papers that he was afraid to do more than lift the boxes on the truck we'd borrowed from one of the neighbors.

"Hey, little bit, you ain't got to be so hard on a brother. I ain't broke nothing and I ain't done nothing to you." He paused in between hauling our television, balancing it on an unsteady leg, eyes fixed on Nona, who returned his half smile with mean eyes.

She faced the grown man and answered him, moving closer

as if daring him not to take her seriously. I knew she wanted to fight. She wanted him to step closer to the line.

"All we need you to do is load the truck. And load it quick. That way you get your ten dollars and we get outta here. Okay?"

I felt sorry for him. He nodded and pushed the television into the truck and didn't say anything else for the rest of the time he worked. When they finished he was the first to take his money and go down the block, moving his feet like he couldn't shuffle fast enough, Afro pick bobbing in a nest of uncombed hair. I was close enough to hear Nona mutter, "Stupid mother-fucker," as he walked away.

Before we left, I stood in the parlor and stared at the nail marks on the floor, squeezing tears out, wiping my face. I looked up when Theresa cleared her throat. She and Mama stood together by the door. Mama ran her fingers over the dark wood paneling; Theresa had her arms around Mama's waist, trying to hold on to her, moving with her like they had three legs. Finally, tired of being so close to anyone, Mama pulled away and headed for the door. Nona was waiting on the stoop. She did not want to say good-bye to the house.

"Are you all right? You were crying," Theresa said.

"I'm all right."

"We're gonna miss this place."

I was angry. Theresa made you not want to say anything. She always got to it first. I shrugged and went out to join Nona. Theresa stayed until Nona opened the door and hollered that we were leaving and Theresa "had better bring her black ass on if she wanted to ride."

I couldn't tell if Theresa had cried or not. She took a seat with Mama, holding on to her tightly again, eyes straight ahead. We traveled so slowly that people must have thought we were in a funeral. No one came out to their porch to tell us good-bye.

But that was all right by me. I wouldn't miss the Sanders

family, who lived two doors down. They had a son with a big Afro and freckles on his face, who smiled at me sometimes and made me almost sick up when he talked to me because I liked him so much. And there was the Jemison family, who had a big dog that had once knocked me down and made me crack my head on the pavement. Mama had had to rush me to the emergency room at Baptist Memorial on Linden Boulevard, where she worked. And there was Tony, CeeCee, Lefty, Barry, and all the other kids that we had played with growing up. None of them even peeked out their window. I took a deep breath and then let all the hard feelings out of my stomach. I didn't have time to be thinking about them—we were moving.

I thought about my favorite game, Hot Peas and Butter, and how I loved to play it more than any other game we had played in the streets. I loved it more than skully, more than handball, and even more than Mother May I. It was the running and then the screaming when someone found the rope and started trying to catch legs and butts, swinging it so hard that it whistled and cracked through the air, making it sound like the beginning of *Wagon Train*. I loved playing Hot Peas and Butter.

I remembered the time Short Sammy had pulled my hair so hard that he made me cry. Daddy had seen it and made me cry again when I got inside.

"That boy half your size and you crying? You should've knocked him down. You come in here again crying like that, I'm gonna give you something to cry about."

I hadn't been able to tell Daddy that I was afraid of the boy, that he might have been half my size but his meanness made up for him being smaller. Daddy wasn't the listening type when it had to do with certain things.

The next time the three of us had been outside jumping rope, Short Sammy came up on me again and was ready to hit me. I closed my eyes and waited for his fist, and when nothin' came I was surprised. I opened one eye. He'd seen Nona and tried to back off, almost running. That didn't stop her, though. She ran, jumped on his back, and sank her teeth into his neck, drawing blood. Theresa screamed, and so did Short Sammy, like the pussy he really was, and people came running.

And there was Daddy, pausing for one moment before he pulled Nona off the boy. In all the confusion only Nona and I heard him as he pushed us inside the house, knowing he was going to have to deal with Short Sammy's mother. "Good job," he'd said to her, "good job."

I opened my eyes wide so the memories would stop. Too hurtful to think of the past, to think of Daddy, the neighbors, and having to leave because he'd left. I didn't understand why I wasn't angry with him. There was still a spot underneath my breasts, right in the middle of myself, that hurt every time I thought of him. Maybe there was no room to be angry because the hurt took up all the space.

We moved to a project building in Brownsville less than five miles away from our old house. Mama told us that five miles wasn't a long way away. That might have been true, but staying in the projects was a long way from living in the house we had grown up in, among the people and the ways we were used to; the projects were not our world.

I was too ashamed to tell people that we stayed in a two-bedroom apartment with stained yellow linoleum instead of hardwood floors. And that we had to set off a roach bomb every day for a month because the apartment was infested—we stepped upon piles and piles of roaches and their eggs, hearing the slight crackle when we accidentally crushed a dead body or a shell of a hatched egg.

The stove was so coated with grease that it took us two hours, working in shifts, to find that the original color was avocado. When I rested from cleaning I cried. That night when we went to bed we all cried. I could hear the choking sobs that

Theresa tried to muffle and the angry punches that Nona threw into her pillow.

We'd never figured on it being so hard to handle, even when we were loading all we had on the back of a truck and saying good-bye to the only house we had ever known. A house that settled, a house trying its best to please us and keep us comfortable even when we no longer had a hammer to fix what was broken.

SIX

WE HAD BEEN IN THE PROJECTS ONLY FOR A WEEK WHEN MAMA
sent me to the store to get her some Argo laundry starch. She
had a deep-down craving for some red clay dirt but couldn't
track down any of her friends to send it from down south, and
of course she wasn't talking to her sisters, who might have been
able to get her a bag of it. So she had to settle for the white
chunks of starch in the blue box that said that it was not to be
ingested. One time I read the label to her because I thought it
might make a difference and stop her from spooning the stuff in
her mouth like Jell-O. She snatched the box from me and told
me to mind my own business and that she was allowed to have
some enjoyment in life. I saw her by the kitchen sink, ingesting,
and five minutes later I heard her in the bathroom, farting up a
storm. That's what that starch did to her—it made her fart long
and loud, and it turned her stomach inside out. But Mama was
determined to have it, since she couldn't get clean dirt in New
York City and none from down south.

This was new territory for me, the streets of Brownsville,
since I'd been used to East New York all my life. The streets surrounding the projects were wide, at least four lanes, with few
one-ways and almost no side streets. I felt small in the shadow

of buildings that rose to twenty floors, sometimes higher. And there were so many people walking around, outside and inside our building, lining the streets and the hallways so I couldn't move without asking permission or slipping by with a nod. That was the big difference about living in the projects and living in a house. There were so many people that I didn't know compared to Ashford Street, where I knew everyone.

The babies screamed, the hallways smelled of sweetened puke, and every building looked alike, painted with the same dead tan-gray color that must have been a cheap buy for the Housing Authority. The difference between living in the projects and living in a house was like watching black and white TV and going to the store and seeing a color one. No comparison.

If Nona had been home, she would have streaked down the hallway and run to the store, making me trot after her by telling me that running was the best way to keep your game up. Basketball—that's all she cared about. But she was already at the park, and Theresa had to stay with Mama in case she started slipping out again. So I had to go by myself.

I knew where the store was, roughly—only about three blocks from the corner of Stone and Sutter. There was a big four-lane street that I'd have to cross and a few abandoned buildings on streets that hadn't been carved out as project land.

I walked like I thought Nona would, trying to act tougher than I was because I wasn't sure about the people around me. I had heard too much about people living in and around the projects. Turned out there was nothing to worry about walking the short distance to the store. All I saw were people just like us— poor people trying to take care of their business.

A big crooked sign held up with red crochet thread hung in the front, identifying the building as Jasper's Candy Store and Sundries. Around the sign, green Christmas tree ornaments were stuck on with pieces of duct tape. When I walked inside it was dark like a cave but familiar, because most corner bodegas used low-wattage lightbulbs. But it was the man at the counter who caught and held my attention. His head was bowed over a notebook and he was busy writing figures. He glanced up quickly.

"What you need?"

I was impressed by the waves of darkness on darkness, of the velvety nature of his skin combined with eyes that were lighter than they should have been given the pure blackness that went to the bone in him. He seemed surprised at me too.

"I ain't never seen you around."

"We just moved here."

"Where you stay?"

I told Frank—that was his name, I found out—all the while thinking that I was out of my mind to be telling somebody I didn't know where I stayed. The door opened, and we both jumped at the light that came through the door. He became businesslike then.

"What can I get for you?"

When I told him he grinned and turned around, grabbing a box off a stocked shelf.

"I didn't think you'd have it."

"Too many people come in here all the time asking. Jasper say we got to keep what people asking for."

He rang me up and gave me my change.

"Come back again, okay?"

Before I could answer he had turned to the new customer, and I felt dismissed.

THE MOVE CHANGED US. I PRACTICED THE GRACE OF KWAI Chang less and less, the pallor of our new walls forcing him to recede. I stopped using my rice paper moves and became like the others, graceless, clumsy, and loud.

There was nothing to fix in the new apartment even though it was dirty. It had a cold feel. There were a few rooms separated by doors, and drafts swept over us at odd moments. Some nights I'd drag out the few tools Daddy had left and pretend to hammer the legs on a table or chair. But no one else wanted to be reminded of him, and the few times I held his hammer were not enough to bring him back. The tool had lost his scent—was he coffee or the smell of sawdust mixed with resin? I couldn't remember.

I searched for Daddy, but he was elusive, a genius at disappearing as well as solving enigmatic problems like rugs out of place.

SEVEN

ONE MORNING, RIGHT BEFORE I WAS LEAVING TO GO TO school, Mama grabbed my arm. Her eyes darted around the living room.

"Where them other two?"

"Nona gone. Theresa in the bathroom. Look, Mama, I gotta go or I'ma be late for school."

"You can't go to school. You need to go get your daddy. Tell him it's time to come home."

"Mama, I don't know where he is. . . ."

"Girl, is you stupid? I'm sending you. I know where he is."

I'd been walking away, snatching my arm from her and heading to the door. My fingers were on the knob when what she said hit me.

"You know where Daddy is?"

"Course I do." She was back close to me, and her nails dug into my wrist this time, making sure I didn't move away. As she whispered I had to turn my head. She hadn't bothered to brush her teeth, but she wanted to be close on somebody.

"Mama, you gotta take care of your teeth. And there's some Listerine in the bathroom." She stuck her tongue out at me as I closed the door, holding my breath. She could've knocked out a horse.

Kwai Chang joined me in the elevator.

"Do you intend to seek your father?"

"I don't know."

"Why would you not?"

Someone came in, and I couldn't answer. But Kwai Chang had said what I was thinking. Why would I not seek my father, the man whom I missed and loved?

I waited at the place where Mama said he worked. He was using his carpentry skills to renovate a burned-out building. Kwai Chang and I marveled at his skills. We peeked in the windows, touched the wood frames, admired the color splotches he'd tested on the concrete front. *My daddy is an artist,* I told myself. Our fingers caressed the intricate wood carvings at the foot of the main door.

I didn't want to leave because I had a feeling he was around the corner, lurking, waiting to come forward. He didn't. Kwai Chang appeared unmoved and spoke to me about searching.

"You must not feel discouraged. Perhaps he is afraid to face you."

"Why should he be afraid? He's my daddy."

He lifted his thin shoulders in a shrug and picked his hat up from the front steps.

"Where are you going?"

I was irritated. I wanted to stay. Maybe there was a chance he would come. Maybe.

"Pamela, are you sure that this is a home that your father is working on? Are you sure that your mother is correct?"

Him asking so soft and without any blame in his voice made me think of crying, but I wasn't in a crying mood.

"Why didn't you say that before if that was what you were thinking? We didn't have to stay here all damn day."

"Would you have listened earlier?"

There is something about being wrong and somebody else being right that can piss a body off. I started walking fast. I wanted to outrun Kwai Chang, the logic that had brought me to the house, and the logic that was making me leave.

"I wish you would stop this shit."

He was at my side.

"What shit?"

I stopped in the middle of the street.

"Either be on one side or the other. Don't tell me to go searching and then tell me there's no hope, that I should give up. You're not being a friend."

"And you have not heard what I said. You heard what you desired me to say. I believe it is time for me to go."

Under my breath I said, "Well, go the fuck on, then."

"I heard that," he whispered in my right ear as he shimmered out of sight.

After he left and I calmed down I decided I must be like the craggy-faced man and travel alone. As Kwai Chang had moved through the arid desert of the American West, I would move through the equally desolate ghettos of Brooklyn, and we would each search: he for his family and I for my father.

MAMA OPENED THE DOOR WHEN I GOT HOME.

"Did you find him?"

"Mama, he wasn't there."

"She been waiting by the door all morning," Theresa said as Mama's fingers slid to her side and her chin dropped to her chest. My mother was an old woman walking to her chair, her shoulders bent into her body, her feet unsteady.

"Pammy, are you sure you stayed long enough? Maybe he was coming from another job?"

I went to stand in front of her. I watched her agitated hands as the thumbs moved slowly around each other in a circle.

"Mama, he wasn't there."

She didn't say a word for the rest of the day, just sat with her thumbs playing war games and her body slumped as though all the air had been siphoned out. Theresa and I whispered together at the kitchen table and spoke about how it was so unbelievable to us that she still loved him even after her divorce, even after not hearing from him in over a year. We shook our heads. What I did not tell Theresa was that I still loved him. That I still wanted him too.

EIGHT

It was Saturday morning and the Duffield in downtown Brooklyn was running a special showing of all the *Planet of the Apes* movies. We wanted to see them, were dying to see them except for Mama, who shook her head at the thought of leaving the apartment. And if she didn't go, that meant that somebody needed to stay with her. Those were rules, enforced by Theresa the Terrible.

Nona kicked the end table nearest her and cursed when she hurt her big toe.

"How we not gonna see them apes? We gonna be the only ones ain't seen 'em."

Theresa sighed.

"Y'all go. I'll stay with her."

"Naw, naw, you stay with her all the time. I'll stay." I tried to sound as if I meant what I said, but a whiny note crept into my throat and I had to look at the floor because my eyes were watering up. I wanted to see the apes.

We had just moved and Mama wasn't too keen on us going outside like we used to when we had a house of our own. Not that we wanted to be in the streets anyway. Project life was different. I felt too close up on people, as though they heard my heartbeat at night and smelled the stink when I went to the bathroom.

At the elevators I nodded and smiled at the neighbors, but I knew who fought and who beat their kids and who screamed at the television on wrestling night.

Theresa sat while Nona continued her obscene tirade. No one else in our family cussed like Nona. I sat back and listened to her, proud of her creativity.

"Goddamn bitchin' mutherfuckin' table." Her face screwed up, her lips drew together, and her eyes shone when she cussed like that, happy to let the words work themselves through her system. When Nona paused in her attempt to enlighten us with the Spanish version, Theresa inhaled loudly to get our attention.

"Y'all know, there is a way to do this an' we can all go to the movies together."

"Like hell," Nona replied, staring at Theresa.

"Mama just got some new medicine," Theresa said cautiously.

It was a simple statement, but Nona and I didn't understand.

"Maybe we could give her some before we go to the movies. You know how that stuff do her—make her sleepy and all. We can give her a double dose an' wait for it to work an' then go on to the movies."

I knew the words were an effort for her. I think out of us three, Theresa took after Daddy the most because she didn't talk much. Sometimes she would go days without saying anything. Her eyes spoke for her, and her lifted eyebrows communicated just the right way. She was the oldest, she was the boss, and we did what she said to do, whether she spoke it or stared it.

"How you know a double dose ain't gonna kill her?"

Saying it aloud, as if we were going to do it, made me feel giddy. We used to be good girls who always tried to be quiet and moved in silence because that's what Mama and Daddy said. But in the middle of the projects things were different. We dared to think of doing what we never would have thought of before.

"It ain't."

There was no other explanation, but since it was Theresa, I knew she had to be right.

Nona finally spoke.

"How you gonna do it?" Nona was watchful, her eyes darting from one big sister to the next, ready to do what we all knew was wrong.

"I'ma put it in her tea. Y'all jus' stay here an' I'll take care of everything."

Before Theresa left, I touched her arm, and she stopped.

"You sure it ain't gonna hurt her?"

She wasn't certain but wanted some freedom from an afternoon of taking turns with Mama to make sure she didn't burn the building down and watching her as she watched old black and white cartoons in the living room.

"It ain't gonna hurt her. She jus' gonna sleep, that's all."

When Theresa left, Nona jumped on top of her bed and began to chant.

"We gonna see them apes, we gonna see them apes."

It was not until we heard the low, steady whistle of the teapot that Nona climbed off the bed and started to act like she had sense again.

DOWNTOWN BROOKLYN WAS FAR BUT WE HAD TO WALK BEcause we had money only for the tickets and for one soda apiece. Nona said that we should take extra money from Mama's pocketbook, but Theresa shook her head, and that was the end of that.

Everything would have worked out fine if it hadn't started to rain. Kwai Chang danced in my head, a slow revolution with his face set, and turned coldly away from me to show his displeasure about how we had done Mama. I shrugged every few minutes or so, hoping the rain would stop, but it didn't, and neither did my guilt.

Seated in the theater, I watched as the Chinaman shook the water from his stringy hair and deposited his barefoot self into the cushioned seat in front of me. He was going to spend time with me today. At first I was bothered by his presence and kept looking at him, but then I lost myself in the apes, and for the next few hours I belonged to them.

Everyone I saw in the theater was black, and to a one we considered the apes black. No matter how much we liked Charlton Heston, deep down the apes were our heroes. I especially liked the woman chimpanzee when she told Charlton that she wanted to kiss him but he was "so damned ugly." Everybody cracked up over that one.

At the end of the movie, Kwai Chang made me notice him by staying at my side instead of disappearing. Now he stood with his goofy, tattered hat as if prepared for the rain on the way back home. In the lobby guys were laughing, imitating the lurching gait of the apes, and everyone was talking, waving, greeting each other. The three of us, four with Kwai, huddled together and felt alone.

"Girl, I didn't know you was gonna come to no movie. I woulda called you."

"Man, that was some heavy shit. Them gorillas was not playing."

"Naw, man, I liked-ed them orange ones the best—they was the best-looking."

Conversations passed over our heads, and I felt we were as invisible to other people as Kwai Chang was to everyone else. I wanted to walk faster and get home. It dawned on me that I had no friends other than my sisters and my mom and Kwai, a man from my dreams. I was embarrassed.

THE LOCK ON THE APARTMENT DOOR TURNED SLOWLY AND made a grinding noise when Nona pushed it open. Theresa rolled her eyes since we had been trying to be as quiet as possible. I thought right away that I would check my toolbox to see if I had any four-in-one. I'd lubricate the lock and doorknob and get rid of that sound. Funny how I knew what to do with problems like doorknobs or dripping faucets without thinking hard. In my mind I could see exactly how I would approach a problem like that, what tools I'd use, and how long the job would take, all in a few seconds. Maybe that was my talent, fixing things like Daddy used to do. That made me smile a little inside.

Mama was not asleep. She was standing in the middle of the living room buck naked, twisting plaits of her hair around her index finger. A frown creased her brow, but it left when she saw us standing in the hallway. When she started to walk toward us I had to turn my head. I didn't want to see her belly bounce or her breasts move from side to side. All I wanted was a normal mother, one who greeted us at the door with cookies or brownies for a snack like the mother from *Father Knows Best*. Even a mother like Lucy Ricardo, crazy as she was, would have been better than this big black naked lady who stood in front of us, showing us a body she should have been trying to cover up.

Although I didn't want to, I finally looked at Mama. She filled my line of vision with her girth and her need to be seen. She had been slender once, but old age had caught up with her to make her forty-three-year-old body sag. The flesh that hung from her stomach and arms was dimpled, and there were streaks across her lower abdomen, lighter in color than the rest of her, ending right above her navel. And then I had no choice but to see my mother's cunt, the place where she and Daddy had made us and where she had finally pushed us out, give or take a few inches. It was bushy with curling gray hairs, and I stared at it wondering if mine would look the same in thirty years.

Theresa didn't hesitate and didn't look away from Mama's bouncing tits and belly. She hugged her and put her arms around Mama's shoulders and led her into the back bedroom, all the while murmuring things in Mama's ear that made her giggle. I only heard, "Hey, Mama, ain't you just a little bit cold running around here with no clothes on?"

"No, I ain't a bit cold." Here she turned serious eyes up at Theresa. "I jus' thought I'd lost y'all and was about to go outside and look." Here her voice dropped lower as if she and Theresa shared some private memory. "You remember the last time, when we went to Coney Island and Pammy got lost?"

While I closed the door, Nona followed them into the bedroom, and I heard the three of them talking, Nona trying to be as kind as Theresa for once. But I didn't want to be kind. I stood in the living room and wanted to punch the television or kick something. There was a heat in the pit of my stomach, and it seemed as if I might explode in minutes. My fingers had curled into fists when Theresa called me from the bedroom.

"Hey, Pam, go and turn on the shower for Mama. She gonna get clean an' go to bed."

And that was all it took for the mad anger to leave my middle: Theresa's voice sounding like Theresa. She was in control, and it made me feel better to know that I didn't have to do anything but what she said.

MAMA WAS IN BED, LONG BURNT-ORANGE FINGERS RESTING on a whiter-than-white sheet, her nails slightly yellow, her arms across her middle, and her mouth open and snoring loudly. Nona laughed at the deep gasp of air that broke through her mouth, but Theresa frowned and went to stand near her head, nodding at me to join her.

"Maybe we can turn her over. Then it won't be so loud." That was me talking, and I jumped at the next breaking grunt.

"Nah, she might wake up. I wanna make sure that she can breathe all right." Theresa straightened the covers and lifted Mama's hands from over her stomach and placed them at her sides.

"At least that look better. Now she don't look laid out."

Leave it to Nona to say that. If it hadn't been for the loud, belly-moving snores that rose from Mama, I would have sworn she was at the funeral home.

We tiptoed out of the room and closed the door firmly, hoping she would make it through the night without getting up again.

Later we sat together with the television muted, watching, eating popcorn, and not saying much of anything until the commercials came on. I was facing Theresa, and Nona was across from us both. Nona pulled out a joint and started smoking. Instead of giving her the third degree or acting like she thought Mama might have acted if she had been in one of those good moments, Theresa stretched and took a long toke when it was her turn.

After a few rounds, we were on the floor in a circle, talking.

"I don't know how we gonna take care of her," Theresa began. I studied her face and thought that of the three of us, she was the prettiest. The reefer made me choke, and Nona thumped on my back.

"If Daddy came back—"

I don't know how I might have finished if the sound of Nona sucking her teeth hadn't interrupted.

"Girl, you crazy. Always thinkin' 'bout him. He ain't tried to find us, has he? Quit it."

Nona frowned at me, and that made me feel bad about mentioning him. I had never thought that he would not be back—ever.

Theresa took no side. She shifted so that her back was against the sofa, and took a long drag from the joint. Then she passed it to Nona.

"Damn, Theresa, why you gotta get so much spit on it? Ain't nobody wanna smoke nuthin' after you done got it all wet."

We all started laughing hard. Nona sounded pathetic, even to herself.

"I gotta get a job." No sound now except Nona blowing out smoke and the hiss of a bud caught fire.

"We ain't got enough to live on, so I gotta get a full-time."

"What we gonna do with Mama?"

"Have to pay somebody to watch her till you two get outta school. You all can't be playing 'round—y'all gotta come right home."

Her face was blank but not her voice, and I wondered when Theresa had taken over, when she had become the adult. Her eyes rested on Nona, who refused to take in anything but the joint.

"Theresa—you all right with leaving school?" It was a careful question by me, who was always the one being beaten up about questions.

Passing the joint to me now, she nodded as the smoke poured from her nostrils.

"Yeah. It's all right. School ain't exactly my favorite place to be." She leaned forward, staring me in the face. "That don't mean you ain't supposed to go. You an' school made for each other. You gotta finish."

Nona giggled and nodded but did not join in our conversation. She was studying the static on the television set.

"You the one readin' all the time. The one talk so proper we ain't half know what you saying. You gonna go to college too, I'ma do that for Mama. And for you too. Even if you don't like it."

When we were finished I picked up the rolled towels from

the door, Nona cracked a few windows, and Theresa picked up the papers and the reefer.

ROLLING JOINTS IS AN ART. THERESA WAS THE FIRST IN OUR family to acquire the skill, and in turn she passed it on to me. Soon I became the official joint roller for the sisters.

I sat for hours learning to regulate the amount of spit on my tongue, to force my thumbs and forefingers to move with delicate intent until I'd made the perfect replica of a cigarette. Not too bulky in the middle, enough reefer spread out so that you didn't smoke only paper at the end. It took me a few weeks, but with practice I learned how to roll a joint that made us all happy.

After Theresa found a job, we started to smoke joints on a regular basis, Thursday and Friday and Saturday nights. Nona and I would rush home and throw our books in the kitchen and tell our neighbor Mrs. Thomas that she could go home because we were in for the night. Then we'd roll a big one and sit and wait for Theresa to get home. We wouldn't start without her.

Some nights before she hit the door good Nona and I would scrunch up our noses. Theresa had taken a job at a seafood processing plant, and she smelled of rank fish no matter what she did. Hours in the tub with a bar of Ivory Soap produced no results other than dry skin that peeled and cracked and still smelled.

One Friday I held a joint while she puffed it and soaked in a Palmolive bubble bath. She took a long toke and held the smoke in for a minute before whispering it out. Nona was sitting in the hallway, propped up next to the door.

It took a few minutes before Theresa started to get a dreamy expression on her face, the frown loosening and falling from her brow. She looked twelve again.

"I hate this job, you know." There was no animus, only a matter-of-fact statement.

"I didn't know."

"You musta knew. Who the hell wants to smell like pussy all the time?"

Nona rolled on the floor, holding her sides. Everything was funny when she was high.

"You don't smell like that all the time." We were down to the nub, and I was trying to work the joint so that Theresa could get one last good puff.

"Right, right. Look, hold the shit still so I can get it."

"We need to get a bong."

"When I get paid next week we'll see."

When she leaned back and gave me the signal that she didn't want any more I relaxed near the edge of the tub and sat. I took one last drag and put the roach in the ashtray. I think we fell asleep.

Theresa woke us up. It was around midnight and she had a pillow in her hands, roughly beating us to bed. She seemed mad too, the reefer only momentarily relaxing her from her boss position.

"That's why you gonna go to school. You ain't working in no goddamned fish factory smelling like fuckin' Charlie Tuna every fuckin' day of your life." She hit me full in the face with the last pillow thrust, and I fell back into the bed and didn't bother to move until morning.

OUR DAYS WERE THE SAME FOR A LONG TIME. NONA AND I WENT to school and came home to watch over Mama, who sat in front of the television nonstop. On weekends we smoked weed and ate like crazy. We took turns going to the grocery store and lived on Ding Dongs, Twinkies, and SpaghettiOs. But we were careful with Mama and fed her the toast she liked and as much tea as she wanted. We bought TV dinners and let her eat them as she watched her shows on television. She still liked *Jeopardy* and cartoons.

To me, things weren't bad—sometimes there was a flutter in the pit of my stomach, and sometimes I thought about Daddy and wondered where his hammered fingers were, but that was only once in a while. The mornings when I woke up with him on my mind were fewer and fewer. And Kwai Chang with his sadness couldn't reach in and pull at my heart anymore either. I was alone in the world with my two sisters and a crazy mama. Tripping off them and smoking some good stuff was all I figured I needed.

NINE

THERESA CAME HOME ONE FRIDAY NIGHT AND THERE WAS A difference. It wasn't that she didn't stink—the smell swept through the apartment as soon as she opened the door. Nona messed with her by holding her nose, and Theresa pretended to ignore her until she got up real close, and then she swatted her across the head with the newspaper she had. That's when I knew there was something going on because she was playful. The way she held her jaw was more relaxed, casual. And she was smiling, her small white teeth showing.

"Y'all, I gotta date."

Nona sat and stared.

"A date? You mean with a guy?"

"Um, yeah. Would you think I'd go with a girl?"

Before she could hide it from me, Nona blinked and got a hurt look in her eyes. But this time I wasn't so much interested in shielding Nona from being hurt as much as I was in finding out about this guy. None of us had ever talked about boys or dating or anything else. It hadn't crossed my mind that Theresa might want to go out with anyone.

She started to fill us in right away, as if she wanted to keep us from asking questions. His name was Danny and he worked unloading the trucks of seafood that came into the plant every day. He lived with his mother and two sisters not too far from us, and they had a house.

"He got any kids?" Nona couldn't help it. Sometimes she asked things to hurt people. Other times, I knew, it was only for the knowing—she liked information. This time I was sure it was to make Theresa feel bad because Nona had never had a date.

"How she gonna know something like that right off the bat?" I turned narrowed eyes on Nona, and she backed off.

Theresa shrugged. "I didn't ask him if he had any kids. He asked me to a movie tomorrow night, that's all, and I'm gonna go."

"Who gonna help us with Mama?" Nona again, being spiteful, not looking to see how she was making the good mood lift from Theresa's face. She pissed me off.

"We can take care of Mama. We do it all the time. Ain't no problem, Theresa, you go on out and have a good time."

"If y'all think you can't handle her . . ."

"Nah. We got ya covered. You go out."

"I was thinking, maybe I could get me a dress, go up on Pitkin . . ."

Nona sucked her teeth and walked away muttering about dresses and men. I stayed and smiled at Theresa, and she took my hand and some of the grin came back.

"Would you come with me to pick out a dress? We won't be long, and Nona can watch Mama."

I had to smile at her because Theresa looked all wide-eyed like one of the Brady sisters. I had my doubts as to my ability to help her pick out a dress, but when she looked at me like I was important, I was sure going to go and do my best.

"Yup. Let's go get you a killer dress. It'll be fun."

She smiled deeper and wider than I had seen for a long time.

PITKIN AVENUE WAS AWASH IN VIBRANT COLORS ON TOP OF the gray, dingy ones we saw every day. It reminded me of a good-looking woman who didn't like to bathe—deodorant on top of funk.

We took the Pennsylvania bus, the number 14, to Pitkin Avenue and got off on the corner where the bus turns wide and stops at the bank, a watered-down used-to-be-white building now chalky with pigeon shit and God knows what else streaking the building. I used to wonder why they didn't at least wash the steps down and put the empty bottles in the garbage until one morning I took the bus early—it was nearly five a.m.—and I saw a man standing with a hose and another with a broom. And then I understood that even though the lady bathed, the traffic in and out of her thighs every day left her just as funky as when she started out.

When we walked into a small store on the corner of Pitkin and Dumont the salesgirl came forward right away. She was Puerto Rican with long hair gathered in a ponytail, talons at her sides, and a hesitant smile on her face. We tried to walk past her, but she followed us through the racks trying to chatter and not act like she was keeping us from shoplifting.

"What you think about this?" Theresa held up a red dress. It was knit and low-cut. I shook my head, and she started to laugh.

"Girl, you gotta wear something to make them look."

"He ain't gonna wanna just look with you in that."

"Guess you right. Anyway, we only goin' to the movies. I'm thinking about a pair of jeans and a nice top."

All the while we were talking, the Puerto Rican girl stood near us with her hand over the metal rack, not even trying to hide the fact that she was watching. A man from the back shouted to her, and she answered without turning her head. Theresa rolled her eyes, and I giggled. But her being close up on us didn't make a difference. Wherever we went it would be the same story.

Theresa ended up buying a pair of bell-bottom jeans with a purple top that hugged tight to her chest and flared just below the waist. I thought she looked like Diana Ross and told her so. At home she smiled in front of the mirror, and Nona even managed to grunt an approval. Theresa was on the thin side, but she had these big eyes that made her seem innocent, especially when she was smoking reefer or happy. And now it was a real smile, a smile that showed the one dimple in her left cheek like the one we all had.

At seven-thirty the doorbell rang, and Nona glanced at me. She was lying on the floor, blouse half open, looking at television upside down. Before getting up, I gave her a mean glance, cutting my eyes at her exposed chest and then pointing at her dirty socks on the floor. When she didn't move right away I paused, and in my head I was Theresa and the stare became harder. She almost fell picking up her shit, and I finally opened the door to Danny.

He filled the room, like Fat Albert come to play. Nona stared at him, her face open and incredulous. I led him to the sofa. He balanced, hand grasping the arm, and then sat. The sofa moved, the feet making a groaning sound under his weight. But when he sat I was able to study his face better.

Jowls. They were the first things you noticed about his face. A hangdog, jowly face with dark blotches on each of his cheeks. And he was light. So light that when he caught Nona staring, he started to blush and didn't seem able to lift his head from the middle of his chest. Since I was next to her, I moved my hand over casually and pinched the hell out of her. She jumped, closed her mouth, and stopped staring.

"So, you and Theresa work together?"

I could tell he was miserable. I imagined his discomfort, being so big and not able to relax. His stomach rolled over the top of his pants. And I tried not to think of what he must look like naked and whether or not his johnson reached beyond his stomach.

Theresa entered the room in time to save Danny. She smiled at him, and he struggled to get up and greet her, smiling too.

"Yes, we work together. I told you that," she said to us, and to him, "You gotta excuse my little sisters. They ain't got much home training."

"Oh shit, you is a big boy."

It was Mama. She had been in her room earlier, asleep.

"Uh, Mama, I thought you was asleep."

"Naw, I know *Jeopardy* is on. I wanna see it." But her eyes never left Danny. Up and down, back and forth they traveled, taking his measure like she was getting ready to sew him a new suit of clothes and didn't know where to begin.

He trembled. After all, he didn't know she was crazy. He just knew she was the mama, and I felt for him—that special flutter in your belly when there is a crippled bird you want to help or a kid you might want to stop everybody from hitting.

Mama continued, "What you doing here? Looking for something to eat? Well, we ain't got nothing. All they gives me is some toast and tea. We ain't got no meat, no fried fish, and no Ring Dings, nothing for a big boy like you."

Nona had turned from us with her hands over her mouth.

"Boy, you is big. Got bigger titties than me. See?"

She started to undo her robe, but I snatched her hands before she could and pulled her from the room. Nona gave up and whooped aloud. The last I saw of Danny that night was him standing next to Theresa, out of place and big enough to seem like he covered half the room. Theresa was staring at him, and neither one was talking. I wondered if they were still going to have a date.

DANNY CAME BACK AGAIN TWO NIGHTS LATER. HE WAS STILL shy, still didn't look at Nona or me, and Mama scared him so much that his foot jumped when she was in the room. She stared at him for a minute or two, then wandered back to her room.

"Well, Danny, how was your day at work?"

"It was fine." His chin was buried so far into his chest, his eyes aimed at the floor, that we had to stretch our necks to hear him answer.

"How many trucks did you unload?"

He shrugged. "Don't usually keep count."

I struggled to find something to say, since it had been Nona holding up the conversation all this time.

"Did anything special happen today?"

It was quiet then. So quiet you could've heard a rat piss on cotton.

"No, not really," he said. I almost said "whew" when Theresa came up front. Danny's shyness wore a person out. We watched as he leaned his body back into the couch and positioned his arms to help pull himself up. The wooden legs scraped the floor and the sofa pillows fluffed out again, taking in air as he rose.

Nona was still sitting quietly on a chair, her round head a picture of hospitality.

"I hope that both of you have a pleasant evening."

"Thank you," said Theresa, but her mouth wasn't saying what her eyes were saying. I knew how Big Sister cut her eyes and for what. Danny and Theresa made it out of the door fast.

"What she mad at you for?"

"I was in the stash when she got home and she mad. Say I don't have to smoke all the time. Especially when he getting ready to come over. You ever heard of such stupid shit? T is fine. She could have anybody she want and she bring home elephant boy? Somethin' wrong with this, don't you think?"

By then we had moved to sit in front of the sofa that Danny had flattened with his massiveness. I reached up under it and brought out a double jacket album cover, the Ohio Players' *Honey.* Flipping it open, I started doing my thing, rolling us a couple of joints. Nona went to the stereo and put the album on. We lay back with our heads on the sofa and passed joints back and forth until the music took us somewhere else good. For me, my head spun around Ashford Street, and then I was in the candy store with Frank, the clerk. A beautiful moment happened with me and Frank then, grooving and moving to the music that stayed just beyond our earshot yet filled my soul. *Ah, sweet,* I thought as his lips pressed mine. *Sweet,* I thought as my legs pressed together, and I wished that he was with me so that I might drink in his deep chocolate skin.

When we woke up it was four a.m. and Theresa had not come home yet. We cleaned up and put our stash away and wished we had some cake and Kool-Aid for the munchies. But there was nothing in the fridge, so we had to settle for going back to sleep.

TEN

Nona told me she was a dyke in between gulps of Colt
45 on a park bench in the middle of the projects in Brownsville.
She wore her hair close in those days, sides tight and faded, almost like a boy's but not quite and with little earrings that
Mama had got for all three of us. Nona's were made in the shape
of a crescent moon, and while we sat on the bench together I
caught a glimmer now and again, like the moon was trying to
shine in her ears.

Theresa had small Aztec suns, and I had the Star of David.
Mama had been pleased with herself when she returned from
Pitkin Avenue with her treasures. We smiled at her because she
smiled, and put them in our ears right away as proof we were
pleased. We looked at each other and admired and oohed for a
few moments before going our separate ways in the small apartment.

Mama had been so excited when she first came through the
door, secretive like Christmas, voice ringing out strident and
clear, like in the old days before Daddy left.

"Y'all, y'all, come on in here. Look what I got you."

She made a speech about us being her sun, moon, and stars.

It was corny. We looked down at the floor, anywhere but at her. In the middle of talking she stopped like she had lost her place.

"Oh, never mind. You girls go on outside and play," she said, and sat down at the kitchen table all by herself. I looked at Theresa, and Nona looked at me. We didn't play outside anymore—we were all too old.

As I left the kitchen, I saw Mama lift herself from the table and turn the gas burner on to make tea. She threw out the paper bag and the three small gift boxes that we had left sitting on the table. I wanted to go to her then, to tell her that I loved my Star of David earrings, but I couldn't get myself to move from the doorway. So I stood there, not comfortable enough with my own mother to touch her shoulder and tell her that I cared.

Nona's body was whipcord thin and always tense, as if she strained under some burden, and now, as she turned her deep, mud-black eyes on me, I suddenly realized what the burden was and what it had always been.

"How long you know?"

"Long time."

I sighed because I didn't know what to say next. I'd never had any experience with dykes, and now that I knew my baby sister was one, things were different. I saw her as sexual instead of as Nona. And I couldn't help it—I imagined her lean body coupling with another lean body or a fat one or an in-between one, two pussies rubbing together, heaving and groaning under the weight of being gay. I shook my head because I didn't want to see my sister that way.

I accepted the paper bag when she passed it to me again, gripping the slightly wet neck as I took a nice long swig and wiped my mouth on the back of my hand.

"You ain't gonna freak out on me, is you?" She didn't look at me as she spoke. I only had the side of her face, a profile that remained rock-still except for her lips moving slowly in the dark. The soft breeze that whistled through the trees felt good on my neck. The day had been a scorcher, with temperatures reaching the mid-nineties.

"Naw. I ain't, but you sure?"

I had to ask, and that's when she turned stony eyes on me, the kind that make you shiver when it's not cold. I felt them brush all over, not from judgment but from longing. And I thought the longing was for what I had, a straight pussy and not a twisted one, and I felt sorry.

"I don't ever want no man to touch me." That was said quietly. And I knew that our father still moved us, still affected us, even if he had left years ago.

When Nona stopped taking baths and started to smell, I had to say something. The three of us shared a room, and it got to the point where Theresa and I were holding our breath until we fell asleep. When Nona came in from playing basketball or hanging somewhere on the street, she stripped down to her underwear in the hallway, threw her clothes and sneakers into the room, and left her funky drawers dangling from the first doorknob she came across.

"Nona, man, nobody wanna smell your shit. You need to shower down."

She moved closer to me and smiled because we shared her secret.

"Chicks dig my scent. They go crazy."

I nodded and leaned in closer. Without thinking about it I said, "Ain't nobody gonna want to kiss your nasty ass. Get in the shower."

Her grin grew wider, as if my words hadn't stung but had somehow made her happy.

"I'm getting, I'm getting." I watched her until she got to the shower, her sparse body damp with sweat, gleaming ebony black against the stark white walls of our apartment. I wondered if she had a lover yet; I wondered what they did together and how it might feel to have soft lips press against soft lips and breasts touch breasts. And then I wondered if Mama would snap from her stupor if she knew her baby girl liked girls.

CHANGE CAME FAST TO US LIVING IN BROWNSVILLE, LIVING IN the projects. We didn't become bad overnight, we didn't drift from each other, but things happened that left us adrift—that made us transition from a family unit to a group of women who lived together.

It was a Friday, and when we got home Mama was waiting at the door with her hand out. She was like that sometimes, wanting money one minute and then asking for a piece of candy the next. We went along with any mood. When it was about money, we knew that Theresa would get involved, telling Mama that she would go pay the Con Edison bill and the rent. So we never worried.

My check was $175 and I gave her $150. Theresa's was a little more, and Mama took a little more. But when Nona came home she didn't have anything, and Mama stared at her, confused.

"Girl, where your money? We gotta buy some food and pay some bills. Where your money?"

"I ain't got none." Nona stood in front of Mama, almost half a head taller but trembling like she was scared. I could feel my heart thudding too.

Mama's hand darted up, and it seemed to me that she meant to grab Nona and shake her, but anger got the best of her. You could see it, cutting through the fog she was normally in, clearing her brow. Instead of grabbing, her hand flew open and she slapped Nona with such force that our baby girl fell back and would have hit the wall if Theresa hadn't caught her. But that wasn't the worst.

"I don't know what you're doing, who you fucking that you

ain't got no money, but you bring your black ass in here again on payday without some money and you gonna be on the street."

There was silence. Not one of us had ever heard Mama use words like *fuck* or *ass*. And she was menacing, body rigid and chest heaving.

Nona cried, big tears falling from her cheeks, but no sounds came from her mouth. It was as if someone was painting a still life of us—Theresa with an arm thrown around Nona's shoulders, Mama standing back but within slapping range, and me cowering from them all because I couldn't believe this was happening—that Mama was hitting and cussing, that Nona was a dyke, that we were all falling apart, and that Daddy was still gone.

We stood there forever, breathing, each afraid to say more because things might escalate, catch fire.

Then Nona moved. She straightened and brushed Theresa's arm away. That meant that she faced Mama square on, and the two of them stared for a few moments before Nona turned her back on Mama and walked away. Mama dropped her head. Theresa followed Nona out of the room.

"Mama, why? Why you gonna hit Nona like that? Why you do that?"

The way I asked it, the words were not sassy. But Mama chose not to answer anyway. She shuffled toward the kitchen, and for the first time I noticed the gray that had once salt-and-peppered her hair was now much more salt than pepper. I heard the cupboard doors slam and the sudden flow of water into metal.

And, of course, unbidden, the Chinaman came to mind. I saw him bow, turning the corners of his mouth up at the ends, gravely because he was not used to joy. And there was a lesson on his lips, but I thought that I should not be seeing him anymore and I refused to listen, dismissing his presence because I was no longer the little girl who loved him and wished to be his daughter. When he bowed and disappeared, I headed to the bedroom to see Nona.

"I shoulda just kicked the bitch's ass." Nona was pacing back and forth in the small bedroom, tears falling more freely and her voice raised barely above a whisper. Theresa sat and watched. When Nona tried to get to the closet to drag out a suitcase, Theresa stood and blocked her way. Nona turned an angry face toward our older sister.

"You need to get outta my way. Just move."

"I ain't."

"Let me go, I gotta get outta here."

"You ain't got no place to go."

As I stood watching them I let out a breath. This was a big relief. I hadn't known Theresa might intervene; I had thought we might watch Nona go without saying a word because we seemed to be the kind of family to do that, to let someone go because it might take too much emotional energy to beg them to stay. We were uncomfortable with emotional energy.

Theresa was only a hair wider than Nona and not much taller. Her features were softer, more appealing. She favored Mama, with curling hair that stopped at the end of her neck and clear skin that did not blemish like Nona's and mine. Now, instead of being overly excited or emotional, she was placid and laid an arm around Nona's shoulders again, as she had done to protect her earlier.

"Look, Mama was wrong to slap you. Dead wrong. But you know she ain't right in the head, and you know you got to bring the money home, girl. Why you gonna go givin' it away to some man?"

I knew better than to say anything, and the three of us sat for a while, each of us trying not to look too hard at the others.

Theresa sighed and stood up from the bed.

"Girl, you got to learn about men. Don't be givin' your

money away." When she left, I sat near Nona and was surprised when she laid her head on me and started to cry in dry, heaving gulps, making small noises in the back of her throat. At first I didn't know where to put my arms; I'd never held her, never felt her flesh next to mine except for the usual childhood hitting and wrestling. Now I held my sister, rocked her, let her snot and tears drench my shirt, touch my skin and my heart.

WHEN I FINALLY WOKE UP IT WAS BECAUSE I NEEDED TO PEE and I was cold. Even before I knew for sure, I knew. I smelled that Nona was gone, almost like I smelled my father's leaving. But with her it was the absence of scent more than anything else, the special gaminess that was all a part of her, gone.

After I peed and turned off the light in the hall, I went back into the room and sat on the edge of my bed and listened to Theresa snore and the sounds in the apartment for a while.

All places have noises. Even apartments in the projects have squeaks and squeals that become part of the background noise in everyday life. The refrigerator surges to life, the sound of electricity a deep hum. The oscillating fan turns, blowing the same warm air around and around. Clocks tick, slower and more silent in the dead of night than they do in the rise-and-shine mornings. It was late, and I felt sadder than I had in years.

I sat and sat, listening and hoping to hear a turn of a key in a lock or the thud of her footsteps in the kitchen or living room. But she never came home, and inside my chest my heart shrank to a marble, squeezed hard and compact and tight so it couldn't leak any more hurt.

TELLING MAMA ABOUT NONA WAS LIKE TELLING A FIVE-YEAR-old about God. She sat in her favorite chair in front of the television, and Theresa held her hand and spoke softly to her. I sat on the other side and watched everything that Theresa did.

First she tried to ease the remote control from Mama's fingers.

"Mama, I need to talk to you about something."

Our mother turned to Theresa for one short moment.

"Not now, it's time for *Jeopardy*."

And if I had not been hurting so much inside from Nona being gone, Mama might have been funny, gripping the remote with a befuddled brow, looking around vaguely irritated at Theresa and me for disturbing her game show.

"We gonna have to go down to the precinct and file a report."

Theresa finally gave up on Mama. She signaled me into the bedroom with a hand gesture and a suck of her teeth to show her frustration.

"You ain't seen her?"

"Naw, not since she booked outta here. She ain't even called."

I was almost in tears.

"Why don't you go down to the park—you know, where they got them hoops—an' look for her? Maybe she just hanging out for a while. . . ."

I headed for the door, knowing all the while that Big Sister didn't know anything and afraid that she might change her mind and tell me to stay with Mama while she went searching.

It didn't take me long to get to Nona's park. I knew a few back streets and alleys, and it wasn't late or even dark out, so I wasn't afraid to move swiftly through them. It was like taking a deep breath and diving into a pool, walking through the projects. You knew you could make it if you used all your skills and were alert every minute and didn't let your mind wander. Your face had to be game too. Mean, not nice, not open, not inviting. So I thought of sad things and things that made me angry as I walked the streets looking for Nona.

I got to the park and saw her right away, playing a pickup

game with a couple of guys I'd seen around her before. The park—which really wasn't a park—had a chain-link fence around most of it, and I shuffled over to the main entrance with my head down, slinking to the left side because Nona pivoted to the right.

There were other people around, some passing smokes, some with brown bags of beer, and others sitting around talking. Every once in a while somebody said something about a shot or a good steal, but mostly people were hanging out and enjoying the breeze that they couldn't get in their apartments.

On a bench off to the side, a bunch of girls sat chewing gum. They popped it loudly, and the sound mixed in with the music of the silver bangles on their wrists and the *bounce-bounce* of the basketball and the screech of sneakers flying across the concrete court made me think of Kwai Chang. The noise was unbearable—although it did not rise, it was constant, and I wondered how they lived with the drone. And for a moment I heard what they heard and knew it for what it was, the forlorn sound of desert life flowing, settling in its own territory, not railing against it—becoming a part of the dry, parched landscape that was the ghetto.

I didn't go near the girls, although a part of me wished that I could. I twisted the small Star of David in my right ear, stared at the massive gold hoops that dangled from their ears, and wished Mama liked bigger instead of smaller. It was as if I was in a different country, and even if I looked close to the part, I wasn't, and they knew it and I knew it even if an outsider didn't.

I watched my sister on the basketball court, leaning forward each time she got close to the hoop, nearly jumping out of my skin when she made a basket.

"That's your sister, ain't it?"

I had not noticed the girl move up so close to me that she

could have stroked my neck with her tongue. I nodded, turning slowly.

There was beauty in the desert. Rough black beauty, but beauty nonetheless. Her eyes tilted catlike, fitting her face, which was cast like an Asian's dipped in toffee. She flashed white teeth at me.

"She my girl."

There was a full moment's pause while we both let the words sink in. I nodded that I understood, and the smile grew wider and she leaned forward and kissed my cheek.

"That mean you my sister."

Innocence or beauty, I thought as her lips brushed my cheek. Which one was more attractive?

Nona came bounding off the basketball court, her body covered in sweat, and I had to smile because her smell wafted near me again and I felt my sister. She was grinning.

"What you doing here?"

"Looking for you."

Broader smile, and she met my eyes with warmth as she grabbed her girl around the shoulders and moved closer to me.

"I ain't coming back. I gotta take care of Monique. We gonna have a baby."

It was then that I discovered beauty's belly, softly protruding. The girl casually laid her head on Nona's shoulder. I saw a blaze of gold hoop earrings, and there was a soft pop from the bubble gum in her mouth. A free hand started to caress her belly.

"I was young—I thought I liked boys, but now I know better. Nona treat me real fine. She brought me this dress and these earrings."

From the set of Nona's shoulders, I knew she was waiting for my disapproval. Monique stepped away from Nona and modeled her dress, blue with white flowers, and touched her ears, caressing the dangling hoops that seemed painful in her delicate ears.

I cleared my throat.

"Where y'all staying?"

There was no smile this time, only a slow nod to acknowledge our love of each other and my acceptance of the way things were. Kwai Chang bowed to me in my head, showing his approval, and I waited while my sister gave me directions and invited me over anytime. Monique smiled at me and squeezed my hand before we parted, and I knew why Nona had chosen her over us.

ELEVEN

IT WAS A SUNDAY, ONE OF THOSE LONG, BREEZY SUMMER DAYS when we could open the iron-barred windows and let the wind sweep through our apartments. Smells that lingered were blown away, and the dust bunnies that hid under sofas and in the corners rolled over the floors, finding new spots where the wind couldn't reach them. I gave some serious thought to finding a broom, but it was such an effort to work in the heat. Better to wait and enjoy the breezes as they washed over my half-naked body. *Tomorrow I will work at cleaning. Tomorrow.*

The fan was off and so was the small air-conditioning unit kept in the bedroom. Not a hint of dull gray clouds lingered nearby, and there was a deep contentment in our project building. At least that's what I felt riding down in the elevator so that I could sit outside for a moment or two.

I closed my eyes on the bench, relaxing as I sometimes did on the train, when there were so many people around that I knew nobody was going to mess with me. I started counting to myself, letting my mind drift as the cool air touched my arms and my cheeks.

"Hey, Pam."

I opened one eye and then the other slowly, pissed off that

I couldn't enjoy myself, until I saw Nona grinning. She was wearing a T-shirt as usual, her legs thrown over an old rusty bike, jeans rolled up higher on one side than the other, with a loosey stuck behind her ear. We hadn't seen or heard from her in three weeks. I reached for the loosey, and she hit my hand away.

"When you start smoking?" I asked.

"Been doing that too."

"Whatcha doing here?"

"Came to see if you wanna go to Coney Island with me and my girl tomorrow."

There was something about her, the casual lean against the bench, the way her eyes met mine, that told me the invitation wasn't so casual. Her calf tensed on the pedal while her fingers plucked at the brake cable.

"Sure, I'll go with you. What time?"

"See, that's great, see. I didn't think you would 'cause you might not wanna be seen with us, you know, but she said you was my sister an' I should ask."

It was excitement that curved her mouth and made it smile without sneering and made her words believable yet sad at the same time. Since when had we ever let what people thought of us get in the way of being sisters?

"Girl, you are so stupid. What time?"

"Early, meet us at the bus stop at seven."

"Cool."

"We'll bring some sodas and some sandwiches an' stuff. All you gotta do is come."

"Said I would."

I stood up and stretched my arms as she prepared to pedal away.

"You ain't going up to see Mama?"

Nona stopped dead, and I wished that I could've stayed

quiet. Her back and how it got rigid suddenly and how she froze tipped me that she wasn't happy to have me asking her about Mama. But it wasn't fair, I said to myself as I waited, that Theresa and I did everything now and had to hire people when we couldn't. There were some days we left Mama alone and prayed that she would do no more than watch her soaps and game shows on the television.

"Didn't know whether Big Sis would let me."

"She ain't happy you gone but she ain't gonna stop you from seeing Mama, anytime you like. An' you know she don't know about your other stuff either, 'bout you being a dyke an' all or about Monique and the baby. I figure you got to be the one to tell her that."

That's when Nona turned to me, and I saw sweat on her brow.

"She don't know?"

"Nope."

There was a long pause, and then she sighed.

"Watch this damn bike for me, okay?"

I sat back down and closed my eyes again with one handlebar in my hand in case one of the homies tried to borrow it for a quick run.

I could almost see us, Nona, Theresa, and me, running through our old house, jacking shit up, laughing behind Daddy's back when he tried to correct the damage, and crying when he got that black belt with the silver buckle. I wondered what type of buckle Theresa would have for Nona this time.

It was dark by the time Nona came back down and claimed her bike. She didn't say much, and I didn't ask. I told her I'd be waiting at the bus stop, and she mumbled something and pedaled off.

Mama was camped in front of the television giggling at Bugs and Daffy as they chased after each other while Porky Pig waited for his moment. Theresa signaled me from the bedroom and I went on back. She was sitting on the floor, a joint rolled, ready to light up.

"Hey, Mama ain't even in bed yet."

She ignored me and lit up, deeply inhaling, eyes closed.

"Theresa, what you doing?"

She opened her eyes and let out the smoke slowly.

"I figure I deserve a smoke after Nona's visit."

I slid down on the floor.

"You could've told me," she said.

"It was her business to tell."

She finally passed it to me, and I took a long drag too, until my lungs couldn't take any more down and I had to let it out.

"I told her that she and the girl could come live with us."

My buzz hadn't started yet. I was on the ground floor waiting for the top of my head to take off.

"Where they gonna sleep?"

Theresa laughed.

"In here with you. I'll move in with Mama."

"Oh, fuck no. You know they fucking. I ain't gonna be in here with them."

Theresa was laughing so hard she dropped the joint in her hand, her openmouthed braying scattering reefer ashes all over the floor. I picked the joint up and sucked on it, willing the high to pour over me.

"Girl, I'm just kidding. They can have the bedroom because of the baby. You and me, we gonna get a pullout sofa for the living room."

"Why you letting them come here?"

"Nona our sister. She done hooked up with this girl an' they ain't got shit an' a baby on the way. I ain't letting Nona go down like that. We gonna try to do what we can 'cause that's what families do."

She was focused, talking strong, even though her eyes had

the glitter of a far-off reefer high. I nodded in agreement and in respect and let the rest of me relax so I could catch the same train she was riding.

I MET THEM AT THE BUS STOP A FEW MINUTES BEFORE SEVEN, and since I got on first I paid their fare. Nona was grateful; I could tell by the way she didn't mention it. One thing I knew about Nona was that you could wait until it snowed in hell for her to tell you things like "Thank you" or "I love you." She wasn't that kind of girl. And we weren't that type of family.

So I paid and we got off the Pitkin Avenue bus at Utica, took the number 2 train to Atlantic Avenue, and then transferred to the D.

Big difference when we boarded the D train at about 7:45. It was clean and air-conditioned and there was no graffiti. Instead of talking, we pretended to watch the trains whiz by the stations. We made eye contact only when we mistakenly looked in the wrong direction.

I tried out a few opening lines in my head, but nothing struck me as correct. I mean, I didn't think it was all right to ask them about being dykes or being a dyke and being pregnant. And I don't know if there was anything that they wanted to say to me or ask me either. So we didn't say much throughout the whole trip to Coney Island.

Since it was near school starting back, the park was crowded with little kids running around. Every few steps I saw women who were gazing back or trying hard to move forward. They wanted to make sure they didn't lose their children, and there was desperation in their movements, the way their eyes darted back and forth surveying the crowd.

It must have been the way that Mama felt when she and Daddy had brought us here all those years ago and I got lost. The day had been just like this too. Cloudless, with startling bright sun overhead, the type of day that makes you blink and wonder why all days in New York can't be the same and why there is such a season as winter and why it always has to be so gray.

I couldn't remember any other trip we'd gone on as a family, but I remembered this one because it was my fault that I got lost. I was holding Daddy's hand and told him I had to go to the bathroom. Mama and the other two were in front and I heard him call her name, but the pressure in my lower parts had gotten too much to hold and I dropped his hand and ran.

I heard him yell something after me, but I couldn't hear him and think of not wetting my panties at the same time. I held it until I was over the toilet letting the flood of pee come down. I remember being relieved that I had made it in time and that I had not embarrassed Mama or Daddy with wetness.

The water from the faucet was strong and hot, and even though the bathroom was littered with a hundred thousand pieces of paper towel it didn't smell, and I took my time washing my hands under the stream. Mama lectured us all the time about washing our hands when we went to the bathroom. I was prepared to tell the truth this time: *Yes, I washed my hands.*

I went to the doorway of the bathroom, squinting because of the sun, and started looking around for my family. I didn't see them. I walked a few paces, right into the crowd. Still no Daddy. I walked a little more. And more. I was scared by then, a feeling in the pit of my stomach like when I've eaten something bad. And I was hungry, the scent of cotton candy helping to make my mouth water. Every child who passed by me had something to eat clutched in grimy hands—ice cream, hot dogs, Milk Duds.

I started thinking that they had left me, that I would be growing up without a family, my last days spent wandering the streets of Coney Island without money or food.

Tears were pouring from my eyes, but I pretended to be hot and kept running my hands over my forehead as well as beneath my eyes. I was too old to be crying. Daddy said this often; Mama said it all the time.

That was when I spotted Daddy out of the side of my eye. I ran to him. He was all I saw, not Mama, not my sisters. My arms were outstretched and my relief at finding him could not be contained. When I got to Daddy, he smiled down at me and patted my head, sidestepping my arms. Mama pushed him out of the way and gathered me to her, and I felt the hotness of her skin and breathed in the tears that had poured down her face, making it appear sweaty. When I kissed her back, I stuck the tip of my tongue out so that I could lick her skin and taste the salt of her tears, which had a flavor like the ones I'd shed earlier.

"See, I told you we'd find her. Now stop all that crying. We're going to go look at the beach."

Even as she held me I gazed up at him, wanting to see his reaction at finding me, his long-lost girl. But there was none apart from the exasperated tone he was taking with Mama.

"Come on now. Let's get going," Daddy said.

Mama had gotten on her knees, holding me with all her might, not caring about the people and holding up the walking traffic. She slowly stood and took my hand tight in hers and didn't let me out of her sight for the rest of the trip. Daddy held on to Nona, and Theresa walked by herself.

I hadn't thought about the Coney Island trip in years, but now that it had come back to me, I thought it strange, the way Daddy had been. Maybe all fathers acted the same way—maybe they didn't demonstrate their love like mothers. Or maybe it was just our daddy. Maybe he was different when it came to things like children getting lost in the park.

But it all made me remember how grateful I had been that day to Mama—for holding my hand and making my trembling stop. That day I knew for sure that she loved me even if he didn't. And I kept that hidden in my deepest heart because that day I started to question whether he really cared about me, about us, and I don't ever remember finding an answer to that particular question.

This was only my second trip to Coney Island, because even though I went to school out that way, I hadn't ever been again after getting lost.

I noticed the dirt first—there was a coat of it on everything. Then I saw the grinning people operating the rides, the acne-faced teens and near-toothless adults. They were drone people—there was nothing in their eyes as they took the money, no love of their jobs or of the people who were in front of them. But there was something on their faces that I couldn't name. They looked like the people in the housing office on rent day when you tried to explain that you had to be late. And once you'd been through that one time, you never wanted to go to explain again. Never. Because you knew what the answer would be and that no one cared that you and your family would be on the street.

We were walking and looking around us, the merry-go-round sounding like sweet bells in the air and the children smiling over their ice cream and ice pops and cotton candy. The adults, when they weren't weary, had broken smiles, giving and giving things to their precious children, and I was glad there was love somewhere. I hadn't seen it or felt it in so long.

THERE WAS NOTHING ABOUT THE BOY AS HE APPROACHED THAT would have made me look twice. He was average in every way except for his mouth, which was tight and angry. He stopped in front of us and would not move. Nona was annoyed. But when I glanced at Monique, I saw more, felt more. Her hand had moved to her stomach—a sign that she was either hungry or scared. I didn't know how I knew this, but I did, and without thinking, I stepped in front of her, next to Nona, blocking the boy with the thin, mean mouth.

Dozens of people walked past us, and I felt the heat rising from their bodies, mingling with and increasing the outside temperature, which had to be at least a hundred degrees. We had to be the only still people at Coney Island that day. Nona and I glanced from Monique to the stranger and back again, over and over again, before he decided to speak.

"I been looking for you, calling your mama. Trying to find you. Where you been?"

He looked past me and Nona, concentrating on having an angry face for Monique, who cringed against the shoulder that Nona offered her. When Monique didn't answer he seemed to notice us finally, although his anger did not drain away.

"I ain't gonna do nothing to her. She my girl. That's my baby. I just ain't know where she been."

Before I could stop her, put a hand on her arm, make her be quiet, Nona had stepped up to him, in his face like she always was.

"She ain't your girl no more, she mine."

He didn't understand. He was shocked. I could see everything played out on his face and I wished that Nona would learn to stop fighting so hard all the time. She was too much like a boxer, always wanting to throw the first punch and catch somebody off balance.

He thought it was a joke for a moment until he saw Monique place her hand on Nona's arm, and the beginning of his smile disappeared.

"You lying, right? Just fucking around?"

One step closer and they would have been mouth to mouth. Nona didn't move but shook her head. There was no playing.

His hands were clenched at his sides, and people kept moving around us.

"You a mutherfuckin' dyke? You a dyke?" His tone was accusatory, and we all knew that given a chance he would have slapped Nona out of the way and started with Monique, but Nona wasn't moving and neither was I.

He leaned in closer to Nona, but his eyes were on the girl with his baby. They never left her.

"Look here, I ain't playing with y'all. Monique is my woman and that is my baby she carrying." His finger was in Nona's face now, and he might have thought to jab her in the eye and at least make her consider. But my sister didn't move, not one inch, and Monique's nails dug into my arm.

"I ain't playing neither." Nona's voice didn't rise, and she was toe to toe with him, waiting, her long body a shadow of his but tensed, coiled, and ready to rain blows.

I don't know what would have happened then if someone hadn't bumped into the boy and knocked him sideways so he lost his balance and fell. That was all it took. Monique dropped my arm, which was tattooed with tiny marks where her nails had bitten into my skin, and grabbed Nona, begging her to come on. As we passed I could hear the boy.

"This ain't it. This ain't over. I'ma find your ass."

I didn't know whether he was speaking to Nona or Monique.

On the way back Monique fell asleep on the bus clutching a Huckleberry Hound dog that Nona had won for her at the basketball shooting booth. After the encounter we'd tried to go on with our trip and pretend nothing had happened. Nona had been all cool and made five baskets in a row, and Monique had squealed like any other teenage girlfriend with a stomach a mile wide. But here we were now, on the train back to the projects, and I was wide awake and trying to figure out how to talk to my little sister.

"Okay, who was he and what was that all about?"

"You know, it was her old man, her ex. Name of Todd. Wanting to start some shit."

"But I thought he was out of the picture. I haven't ever heard her mention him."

"Naw, I guess like he said, he been looking for her. That's why we're coming back with you all to live. He was coming around to her mama's making trouble and stuff. He ain't wanna let her go."

"Nobody told him about you two?"

"Guess ain't nobody wanted to fool with that."

"Well, Nona, what you gonna do?"

"What I have to do to protect my family."

We were sitting next to each other, and a wide arcing swing of the bus made Nona shift in her seat and slide toward me, so I had to keep her from falling. And I thought again as I hugged her to me for a second that I wished she could leave this girl alone—Monique with the Asian eyes and honey-coated skin, Monique who seemed as though she might melt on my tongue anyplace I pressed my mouth.

"By rights you ain't got no family. That baby's his."

Her eyes were hard.

"The baby is Monique's, and me and Monique is together. I'm not talking about it no more. And don't go telling Danny or Theresa. They ain't fighting no battles for me. I got to deal with this myself."

"Nona," I started, but before I could finish, Monique woke up and stretched her arms and yawned noisily as if she were at home instead of on a public bus. Nona turned to her, and I saw that they smiled at each other.

"You had a good nap?"

"Yup. It was real good."

And that's all I heard because I was trying to think about what I could do to help, if I could do anything, and whether it would be a good idea to tell Danny about this whole mess.

TWELVE

I DREAMED OF YOUNG BOYS TRYING TO HOLD ME WITH FUM-
bling hands against the cool tile walls of my building, passion-
ately kissing me before the door to my apartment opened,
Mama facing me or Theresa dressed like Mama facing me. Our
tongues touched frantically with the promise of more later,
more tomorrow. I grew to dislike the vague longing that I felt
between my legs, the light moistness that could not be
quenched even with a pillow or the length of two fingers. Frustration drew me to the decision that older men must be pur-
sued, men with cars, men with apartments and money, men
who might satisfy my curiosity and longings. Men like Frank the
clerk sitting in his dark candy store. Chuckie was long gone. I
had tired of chaste peppermint kisses.

Frank the clerk owned muscles that rippled at his stomach,
and his face was mysterious and filled with lust for my sixteen-
year-old body. I could tell his interest by the way he lingered at
my breasts and by the way his big tongue caressed his lips each
time we met.

When I saw him play handball against the side of the
bodega one day, without a shirt, saw the way his blue-black skin
continued in one long drink to the belt of his jeans, I was fasci-

nated. I stopped to watch, and when he was finished he saun-
tered over to me, smiling. He slipped his shirt on slowly, giving
me adequate time to see what he wanted me to see.

"You outta school early."

"Yeah."

"What you need?"

"Um, just a snack."

The smile was slow and wicked.

"Are you sure that's all you want?"

We had moved to the store, and he was behind the counter.
At sixteen I was unsure of how to talk to a man. I nodded,
placed my chips and drink on the counter, and held the money
in my hand. No one else paid us any mind. When he gave me my
change, his middle finger lingered in the palm of my hand,
scratching, and when I met his eyes, his had darkened and the
place between my legs moistened suddenly.

"When you want something else, you let me know."

Kwai Chang was a sly such-and-such. I had not seen him in
a week, yet as I rounded the corner there he stood in the middle
of a vacant lot, waiting for me. He strode across the litter, bottles, broken syringes, and rubbers and fell into step with me
without regard to his feet, which were, as usual, bare.

He only held his tongue for half a block.

"You are not serious about this man, are you?"

It was summer and not a breeze stirred the air, yet the way
his body braced for my answer, I had the impression that his
weathered skin and half-closed eyes were facing a sandstorm or
hurricane.

"Why do you ask?" I could be as mysterious as he, doling
out questions for answers too.

"I am concerned. I do not wish to see you hurt."

"I can take care of myself, Chinaman. You need to leave me
alone."

"Surely he is not worthy of your love. Did you not hear

what he said to you? As though you were common to succumb to such talk?"

This was the closest to anger I'd ever heard Kwai Chang. He stopped in the middle of the block, and when I glanced at him full in the face there was a weary puzzlement.

"Look, I'm tired of waiting. I want to be with someone. I don't have anyone. Oh, shit, you wouldn't understand."

But I knew he did understand—and he knew that I knew. We were searchers together. That meant that he didn't have anyone either. He stood still for a moment and then bowed from the waist to me, his hair brushing his cheeks, his eyes grave when he opened them again in my direction.

"I must honor this decision that you have made. It is your destiny."

He began to disappear, little by little, into the sidewalk and into the small patches of weedy grass that sprung up in between the cement.

The last I saw of him was his big toe, which for some reason had become the bearer of a used condom, floating pointedly at me. I had to grin. Kwai Chang was going to make sure I got the message.

I WAS IN BACK OF THE CLERK'S BUICK, LEGS SPLAYED, RESTING on the dark fur piece that he kept and wrapped around us for protection. The car smelled of incense, and I closed my eyes to his face looming in front of me, big and distorted, veins bulging from his forehead as he worked his body on top of mine. For a moment I thought Kwai Chang would appear, eyes leering and head nodding, even laughing at my discomfort. But then I knew better. He was a gentleman. He would not show up in this moment of intense heat and witness my rutting with someone else.

Holding my breath, I counted twenty more thrusts, a final heave, and then suspension as he rested a weary head on my shoulder.

"Are you okay?" he asked, and pulled himself from me slightly. I noted that his eyes had refocused, and now he saw me instead of the legs and mound I had represented a moment ago.

I nodded solemnly, and that seemed to affect him too. He kissed the side of my head. That was the first kiss exchanged between us.

"Let me get you dressed and back home."

Still I remained quiet.

As he put on his pants, he added, "Next time, I'll get us a room or something. I just couldn't take you home, you know I got Angie there."

Although it was dark, it wasn't late. We were parked near an abandoned building off Utica Avenue. When Frank the clerk had parked, he'd made sure that I knew he had a gun for our protection and that I could relax. He also told me about Angie, his pregnant girlfriend, and said that he didn't love her. I heard every word he said to me but it was like being in a movie theater, way in the back. The action was up front and I was somewhere drifting.

When I took a bath Kwai Chang showed, his back to the tub, sitting cross-legged. I knew he could not help his desire to be in my presence just as I could not help letting Frank the clerk sex me.

"You are well?"

I listened for any hidden meaning in his voice. Was he jealous? I'd watched him take women on *Kung Fu*. They were always white women whose soft-looking skin belied the tough times of life in the Wild West. The camera became hazy as they exchanged a first kiss, and then there they were, in the barn, in a bed somewhere, waking up. No grunting like Frank the clerk.

"I am fine."

"Do you know the nature of men?"

"Now I do."

He shook his head, scraggly hair floating around his face.

"No, you do not. And that will be a problem for you."

"What do you mean?"

"You will soon see."

Silence. When I rose from the tub and wrapped the towel around myself, he still did not glance in my direction. Instead, he began to disappear, leaving me to wonder why he had come for such a short time and asked about the nature of a man. Was it more than the thrusting and the seeking I had just encountered?

The next time I met with Frank the clerk he rented a room at a Travelodge near downtown Brooklyn. The Friday night crowd wound its way through the lobby and down the hallway, waiting for rooms that were rented by the hour.

I found myself staring at the floor, at the ceiling tiles, at Frank the clerk's hands, anywhere but at the other couples lining up behind and in front of us. It was awful, the way some girls clung, grinding their hips to connecting crotches, darting tongues into hairy ears. If Mama ever regained her mind and found out, she would be angry. Kwai Chang must be angry already.

Frank pulled me close and put his hand on my bottom, clutching me as though he cared for me rather than for my pussy. He rested his chin on the top of my head and then bent to my ear.

"If you want to leave, we can. I don't want you to feel bad."

There was a slow, reassuring smile on his lips, and again I was surprised—by the rise of feeling in my chest, by the depth of kindness in his eyes. Somehow he reminded me of Chuckie, and I forgot about the line of waiting fornicators in front of us and let myself get lost in his eyes.

"You're so quiet. What are you thinking?"

"Nothing."

We stood on line then and didn't say much of anything until we got into the room. And then we said even less, our breath mingled and harsh-sounding. I thought we would look ugly, mouths open and gasping for air, and I stood outside of myself to look at him, at us. But we were not ugly, especially not when we finished. He covered my face with kisses and then took my hand and kissed the inside of my palm, laying his cheek in it for a moment. I felt warm, sleek with his sweat, his body's tears.

They rang the room when our four hours were up, and we dressed fast. He dropped me two blocks from my building and drove slowly beside me to make sure I made it home. When he waved good-bye, my heart thumped a little, and I thought of a long bath to wipe the tears and him from me. I wondered if I loved Frank the clerk.

THIRTEEN

A WOMAN IS A TREE. I CAME TO THIS CONCLUSION AT THREE A.M. after having smoked almost a nickel bag by myself. I still couldn't fall asleep despite the hour and the hum in my head that made me want to crash. I'd read the book *A Tree Grows in Brooklyn* when I was much younger, maybe twelve. There, the girl had a rooted tree, one that reached into the earth and held on with strength and stays, year after year. I saw myself with her kind of tree, my arms spread wide in embrace, my brown skin rubbing against the bark, caressing the outer skin, face-to-face with another woman, a mother woman, who offered me shelter in her strength, in her roughness.

But this strong tree was not the same as the project saplings I saw every day, the kind planted just so the neighborhood wouldn't look as poor, run-down, and beaten as it was. The saplings broke from being leaned on too hard and from being asked to bear too much too soon and to bear it all in silence, the way rage is not to be screamed.

I hadn't seen a tree in the projects that was as strong as the tree that grew in Brooklyn for that girl way back then. But I closed my eyes and imagined, digging my heels into the bed like it was the earth. I promised myself not to sway with every breeze and to stand firmly in one place. And when I made this promise to myself I began to drift, and I fell into a dream of leaves, tree bark, and young white girls looking out of windows.

In the morning when I woke my mouth was dry and my tongue felt heavy, without purpose, and unable to work up a decent amount of saliva to coat it. What I wanted to do was find my stash again and start the day with a joint, just like I'd ended it the night before, but I couldn't bring myself to start so early. It wasn't ten yet.

Sundays had quieted down without Mama playing gospel music loud enough to make the walls sweat and sing with praise. At first there had been relief and then a curiosity and finally a knowing. She'd stopped because things had changed. Monique was here, Danny came often. It wasn't the four of us any longer, and she was confused.

Theresa was on the edge of Mama's bed with a cup of tea and some oatmeal, trying to convince Mama to take a bite or two. But it was one of the days when she'd decided to sit and stare at the wall, and her lips would not open. Theresa took Mama's mood personally and sighed loudly as she gathered up the bowl and teacup and headed for the kitchen. I took her place on the bed.

Mama had beautiful long nails but hands that were rough and worn even though she hadn't washed a dish since before we left our house and moved to the apartment. I picked up her hand and rubbed it against my cheek, and I knew there was a flicker of awareness in her eyes. The other hand rose to my other cheek, and I couldn't help it—I started to cry. I moved up in the bed and laid against her, burying my head at her breast. She smelled of Ivory soap and chamomile tea. She still didn't talk, but she held me—I felt her arms around me, and she started to rock me, back and forth, forth and back. I fell asleep there, and it was the best sleep I'd had in a long, long time.

When Frank the clerk called and asked if I would meet him

at the candy store and go to the ten-dollar-an-hour motel, I told him no. There was silence on his end of the phone and finally defeat in his "All right."

I felt bad for a while, and there was a part of me that wanted to go to the store and see his dark-skinned face again and touch the muscles at his stomach and feel that he was in some way mine. But that part was put away when I heard the cries of a little baby girl in my mind—the child he created with Angie, the one balled in the pit of her stomach, the one he had put in her and not in me.

Although he didn't appear with the regularity that he once had, sometimes I was able to conjure the Chinaman with a thought. He stood next to Frank the clerk, who slowly vanished, and there was a hint of a smile on Kwai Chang's lips, which were not used to happiness.

"I am glad," he said to me, and I nodded, wondering if I truly knew the nature of men now or whether I was running from what I should not know at sixteen. But it didn't matter, because there was sweetness between Kwai Chang and me again and calmness inside my head. I did not have to go to the Travelodge and hide my face in shame or splay my legs in the backseat of a car. I wondered why I'd done those things in the first place. I was puzzled for a while, but then I let it all go in relief.

"Never again," I promised myself and Kwai Chang, "never again."

A GIRL WHO LIVED ON THE SAME FLOOR AS US STOPPED ME BEfore I got on the elevator. She was my height but heftier, and her arms were fat hams with raised scars spiraling around and around. Her eyes dipped at the corners, and she would have been pretty if she didn't look so hard. Mean as the streets, the color of worn black tar.

"You done heard Frank in jail?"

Girls here wouldn't look you in the eye. We had to look

everyplace else—the elevator button, the graffiti, the yellow walls. I learned that Stuart in 8G liked to suck big dicks. Over the U in his name a penis seemed to squirt red come.

"Naw, I didn't know."

"Police came an' raided the place las' night. They holdin' him at the Seventy-fifth. He told me to tell you."

I finally looked in her eyes and I was surprised because they didn't seem mean. There was some kindness in them, dug out from a long time ago, kept deep inside, but given to me this once.

"Look—if you decide to go see him, you probably should call first. His woman, Angie, she crazy an' she done had the baby. She'd jack you up if you went there when she was there."

I nodded and half smiled and got ready to say thanks, but she turned from me, heading down the hallway on the brown linoleum that shone through the streaks. I pressed the button to go downstairs and take a walk. I couldn't believe that Frank the clerk was in lockup.

I'D SEEN STORIES ON TELEVISION ABOUT JAILS. BUT WITH TV you couldn't smell. The smells were a combination of waters—sweat, tears, piss, and vomit mixed with shit. There was no earth smell, only hard floors, fluorescent lights, and brown—tables, chairs, and people. Frank the clerk had been moved, and when the girl came again to me and asked, I said that I would visit. As I was sitting across from him, I couldn't believe that I was in a jail, that I was visiting a man, my one man—and that it was Frank.

"Time passes slow in here. I think I'm gonna be locked up for a good while. I can't raise no cash and ain't nobody else gonna do it for me."

I was glad that he wasn't upset or whining and that he was matter-of-fact, talking like we used to before we got the sex going between us.

"Do you need anything?" I couldn't think of anything else to say, and I was glad when he shook his head.

"Pam—I just wanted to see you again. Tell you I'm sorry things ain't go the way they shoulda. Probably shoulda left you alone."

"I wanted to too."

He reached over and touched my chin, and I saw regret and hope on his face, like I was there to do more than talk. But I couldn't give him more. He got the picture when I moved my chin away, and he sighed. He tried to hide them, but I saw tears standing in the corner of his eyes. They were deep black eyes, darker, I thought, because he was in that place and everything was harsh and bright. Even his skin seemed darker under the light. There was a gray undertone that made him look sickly. He was not beautiful there, not fresh or strong.

We spoke a little more, both of us trying to hold a conversation, but we were far apart. He was asking me about high school, and I was thinking about how horrible it must be to be locked up with that stench. Our eyes began to slide off each other, and I knew it was time to leave.

He signaled for the guard, and I stood. He took his time and rose above me, and we allowed our eyes to touch in the final seconds of our time together.

"I'm sorry you're in here and I can't do anything to help you."

I hadn't thought I would be torn up about it, but I was, and my voice quavered when I said what I felt. Frank the clerk nodded at me, and the last time I saw him, in his loud orange jumpsuit, he shuffled out of the room, his shoulders back and his head down. He turned and stared, one long gaze without a smile.

Frank was on my mind for a long time. At night I would lie awake, even if I had a joint to help me sleep. Visions of a tall man walking away, swallowed up by the dark, made me rest-less.

I started to read again, for long hours into the night and into the mornings. I read books, newspapers, magazines, anything I could find to try to take the image of his gray-black face away. But then it got worse, and it wasn't just Frank I saw. It was a combination of Frank and Daddy—a bad combination. I'd dream I was with Frank, in the backseat of the car, and suddenly the face would change and hovering over me was Daddy—only there was no pleasure in his face. Frightful tears slid down his cheeks, and with each stroke he murmured, "Sorry."

I knew I was sick then, that sex had made me sick. And I de-cided when I woke up from the dream for a third night, when my body was covered in sweat and I couldn't catch my breath for fear that I had slept with my father, that I wouldn't "do it" anymore. Nothing was worth the picture I had in my head of Frank and my daddy, sharing one body and thrusting between my thighs.

FOURTEEN

IN SCHOOL WE WERE READING *THE SCARLET LETTER*. MY ENGLISH teacher read in a monotone and I could tell that this was not her favorite book, but I liked it. It was about sin, lust, and revenge—the kinds of things that happened in real life and not only in books. I felt like I knew Hester and could feel the weight of the letter *A* on my chest too. But it was a good weight. She had to feel that. Because at least she was being punished for what she did wrong. At least the stuff was out in the open, and she was woman enough to bear that burden and raise a baby too. The minister was weak. And so was the husband, slinking around and acting like he was too good to have ever sinned. By the time we finished reading I was mad at men and couldn't help thinking about Daddy. How he'd taken the easy way out and left us to take care of Mama and ourselves. I thought I would brand the letter *C* on his chest—*C* for *coward*.

FIFTEEN

HIS FINGERS WERE FAT LIKE THE REST OF HIM, STUFFED sausages with skin stretched tight across them—appendages that floated through the air even though they were weighed down by the heavy meat that hung from his wrist. But they danced back and forth over the skillet, alternately stirring peppery ingredients into the eggs and dusting a mixture of cinnamon and powdered sugar over the French toast.

"Onions, you putting onions in those eggs? I don't think I want any."

"Why don't you wait and try them first?"

I had grown used to his voice and the way nothing was ever done fast with Danny around. I knew I would taste the eggs even if I had made that remark, but that was how we got along. I sat in the kitchen with him every Saturday and Sunday morning while he cooked us all a big breakfast. It was my job to hand him things from the refrigerator, mainly because it took so much effort for him to move, and then when he did, the kitchen was too tight for him.

"He need to lose some weight." Mama said things like that under her breath when he was around, but she knew better, crazy as she was, to say anything like that aloud anymore. I think Theresa would have locked Mama in her room if she said too much of anything about Danny. Theresa was in love.

The night they'd had their first date—the night that Mama talked about his titties—I'd thought for sure that he wouldn't come back, but he did. Over and over. It got so Nona stopped rolling her eyes when he knocked on the door and he stopped trembling when he had to spend some time with us. Which was kind of funny, him being afraid of being around us, but that was how he felt. It was easy to see.

It happened that he worked on us gradually.

"We gotta meet." That was how Theresa started all family discussions. Nona and I looked at each other because neither one of us could remember anything we had done to have a meeting. Theresa sat on the edge of the bed, staring at the floor. We waited for her to begin, waited and waited.

"Me and Danny, we been seeing each other for a while, and I kinda wondered if y'all would mind if he spent the night every once in a while."

"What?"

Nona had been sitting on the same bed with me, but when Theresa finished Nona jumped up and got in her face.

"What you talking about—bringing some fat-ass man in here? We don't need no man. You don't need one."

There was a moment when I thought that my older sister would hit Nona and chase her away again. But it didn't happen.

"I do need somebody in my life. And it's gonna be Danny." Theresa picked up her head, and even though anybody could see that she was embarrassed, she faced Nona head-on. "I ain't said nothing about you bringing Monique here. We done gave her a home along with the baby she expecting. All because you say you love her. Well, I'm telling you that Danny gonna come and spend some nights here. He my man, and ain't neither one of you pay no bills."

She couldn't get the words out fast enough, and she choked, gasping for air but even more for understanding.

"I ain't saying that y'all ain't got no say in this. But it's my apartment too—I work hard to make sure we have a place, and I want to be able to bring my man home if I feel like it." She left the room.

"Why things got to change all the time? We don't need no men in this house. We had Daddy and he left. Don't she know nothing? He gonna leave too and she gonna be sitting up here crying."

"Nona, you ain't right."

"Why you say that?"

"Theresa's been on your side and helped you and Monique. You just got to get over your attitude about Danny."

Nona only took a moment to think about what I said and then she was in motion again, stomping out of the room in her size ten Pro Keds. Her body was made to move, to never be still. She had to go pick up Monique at the free clinic. She muttered on her way out that maybe I was right but that didn't make Danny any friend of hers.

THE FIRST MEAL HE COOKED FOR US WAS DINNER. HE KNOCKED on the door at four o'clock on a Saturday, three bags of groceries awkwardly held in his arms and sweat pouring down his forehead like little rivers. I thought at first that he might have climbed up the twelve flights of stairs—maybe the elevator was on the blink. But he hadn't. It was the summer heat and his retained water. At least that was what Theresa explained to us later.

He shooed us from the kitchen, and Nona, Monique, Mama, and I sat in the front room sniffing and listening to the sounds of meat cooking. We had been in the projects for over a year and this was the first time that I recalled having a real meal cooked. Monique kept rubbing her stomach, and Nona wasn't happy as the smells came drifting our way. Mama kept glancing at Monique as though she was still trying to figure out who she was—like maybe she had had another daughter but couldn't quite put her finger on the name. Monique thought it was funny, and she had started to call her "Mama" with the rest of us. I minded, but only because it confused Mama. Nona and Theresa thought there was nothing wrong with it.

We didn't have a dining room, and the kitchen was too small for Danny and the rest of us to get around in at the same time, so when he called us for dinner, we waited until he came out into the hallway and lined up single file with plastic forks and knives and paper plates. He had made biscuits with smothered pork chops, the meat falling from the bones. There were string beans and a big pot of mashed potatoes.

Monique was first in line because of the baby.

"Make sure you get enough there, Monique. You is eating for two."

That came from Danny, standing away from us with a dishrag thrown across his shoulder. He'd never talked like that to us before, and I was curious. Before anyone could say anything else he continued, "You know, you gotta eat healthy now. I got you some salad stuff too. You like tomatoes?"

Monique nodded, and I saw Nona's unreadable face as she bent over the stew pot to fish out a pork chop.

"Look in the fridge. I thought you might like some of that French dressing."

We waited until Monique got her salad plate, and then Danny led her to the table. It seemed right. He sat there talking to her until we all piled our plates high. Theresa helped Mama and then fixed one for Danny. She didn't give him any more or less than anyone else.

It was funny that Mama was so quiet during all of this. She kept staring at Danny and Monique and then dropping her head. She kicked me under the table and whispered, "Who are those people?"

Finally Theresa fixed her own plate and we sat at two folding card tables in the living room. Nona snapped the television off, and we were just about to begin eating when Mama cleared her throat with a loud,

"Ahem, I just wanted to say thank you, Lord, for this here new daughter that I got that I didn't know I had, and thank you for this big boy that done come and cooked for us. I ain't had no real food since we came to stay in this place, and I was just thinking about some pork chops."

We were eating like we hadn't eaten for years. At one point I felt some gravy trickle down my chin, but I didn't want to stop and wipe it off. All I was thinking about was the next bite of meat, the next biscuit I'd grab before Nona got in the way. When I stopped to take a breath I noticed everyone else leaning over their plates with intensity too. I guess we were tired of potato chips and Twinkies.

Mama was going at the food just as fast as she could when she put her fork down with a clatter. It was loud enough to catch our attention, and we all stopped.

"This here reminds me of the time your daddy took me out with him to the pool hall."

Mama had not spoken of him since before we moved.

"I made us all a good dinner that night before we went out. You know, I felt bad about leaving y'all and I wanted to make sure you got a good hot meal. Plus, I didn't want to go spending so much money eating out. We didn't have a lot in them days."

She paused and took a drink of the Welch's grape juice I'd put in her jelly glass.

The only sound was of Nona still eating, pretending to ignore Mama. Monique put her hand on top of hers, begging her to be quiet. Theresa and I gave Mama our attention—we had rarely heard her lucid lately. Danny's mouth was open and he was breathing through it, since his nose had gotten stopped up with all the spices in the kitchen. He breathed like a man on a respirator. I wondered how he was able to lift and load seafood on the big trucks. I wondered how many fish he had dropped snot on. Then I wondered if he had dripped on the pork chops.

"We waited till y'all ate and was ready to go to bed and then we asked Mrs. Stewart to come over and sit. In them days we didn't have to pay no babysitter. We just returned the favor. I put on my suede dress." She turned to Theresa. "You remember that dress, the one with the kick pleat?

"That night Theresa had to help me get dressed. She wouldn't leave the room. And you—" She turned to me. "Oh, God. Somebody would have thought that I was leaving you forever. You wouldn't stop crying. Finally your daddy spanked your bottom and put you to bed." She frowned. "I told him that wasn't a good idea. That he had to speak to you and explain things to you, that you was too young to be spanked and all you wanted was your mama. But he ain't never had no patience. Never."

"What about me?"

Mama smiled at Nona, who had been trying not to seem like she wanted to hear but couldn't resist asking.

"Baby, you wasn't nothing but a baby. Couldn't have been but a year or two. I put you to bed with your bottle and you was hard sleep."

Another sip of Welch's and a soft burp interrupted her story. She covered her mouth and glanced coyly at Danny.

"In China when you belch it's considered an honor to the cook. That's what your daddy used to say. He was in the army and visited places like that. All around the world.

"Anyway, we went to the pool hall, me in my dress. . . . I shoulda known it was gonna be some trouble, but you know sometimes I didn't care about no trouble. Sometimes I just wanted to go out with him to see what he was doing. Follow behind him. But I shoulda known better this time. When we walked in, I was the only lady there."

No one was chewing.

Out of the silence came a deep rumble. Danny had farted. Nona turned her head in disgust. Monique snickered. Theresa ignored him, and I wondered how sick he must be that he couldn't hold a fart at the dinner table.

Mama went on.

"Now, when I say I was the only lady, I don't mean there wasn't no other women. A lot of flat fuckers and hoochies was at the bar. But I didn't see nobody like me.

"Your daddy put me in a corner and left me there for most of the evening. See, he was with his people—he knew everybody in there and I didn't know nobody. He was trying to show me that I couldn't be following up under him. He wanted to make me feel bad."

"What did you do?"

The softness of Danny's voice drifted across the table. His face too was all round gentleness, with traces of embarrassment rolled into it for that awful fart he'd given us minutes before.

Mama turned to smile at Danny before answering.

"I sat there for a long time and didn't do nothing. But then I got mad. And I started smiling at a man across the bar. When your daddy went to the bathroom, the man came on over and introduced himself, and I let him hold my hand long enough for your daddy to see him." She closed her eyes and her head swayed, maybe with the weight of the memory.

"Your daddy picked the man up from the table and threw him out of the bar window. We paid for that for a full year, ten dollars a paycheck. We never went out again—not like that. Never again."

She stood from the table, and I could see from her eyes that she was finished being sane, because they clouded over and her lids dropped halfway.

"I'm tired now. I'm gonna take me a nap. Thank you for this good meal, boy. Now you better go sit on the toilet before you explode."

IT WAS LATE BUT I COULD NOT SLEEP, UNACCUSTOMED TO THE fullness in my belly. Danny had cooked again, some type of stewed meat with carrots and celery. After, we talked and laughed in front of the television, and I imagined that we were a family. I was listening to the sounds in the apartment again—the snores from my mother, the whispered hush of the wind blowing through the barred windows.

Theresa and Danny had long since finished their sex play. The slow moans that shook the apartment each time he spent the night were gone. And I was lonely without the sounds. I couldn't tell if it was Theresa's or Danny's voice or a mixture of the two, twining together in consummation and satisfaction.

Nona always smirked the morning after Danny had spent the night, her standard comment about sleeping well making Danny blush through the yellow hull of his skin and putting Theresa on the defensive.

"As well as you two."

I wondered if I was too old to take comfort in the fact that I was now sleeping with my mother. That sometimes, when she was in a deep sleep and the loud snores pulled from her chest and through her lips, I was glad. I tried to get as close as I could without disturbing her, and I lay awake and listened. I waited for these nightly moments, and I was content.

I fell asleep, and suddenly there was a hand on my shoulder and an urgent whisper in my ear that made my spine quiver. It was Nona, and she had a finger to her lips and a pair of my jeans in her hands that she laid across my body. I nodded in her direction. I understood.

It was long past midnight when Nona and I sneaked out of the apartment to smoke some cheeb—Acapulco Gold, she said it was—and as soon as I inhaled, I knew why they called it that. It felt good going down, smooth, and after about half a joint I waved my hand at Nona, signaling that I was finished for a while.

She kept puffing, never letting the joint go too long without her lips wrapping around it. When she finally paused it was to tell me that she had another in her pocket for later.

It was a cool night in early October, and we were just starting to see fall. An Indian summer, that's what they called this extended good weather. The leaves fell from the trees slowly, and it did not seem as though the grayness of winter was to set in shortly.

As soon as Nona finished the joint and pocketed the roach, she pulled her loosey from her ear and lit up, puffing like she was a chronic smoker. Theresa had outlawed reefer and smoking in the house on account of Monique. Actually, it was Danny who'd said something about all the smoking not being good for the baby, and Theresa agreed. So now when Nona and I wanted to get high, we had to go outside.

On top of everything else, Theresa had stopped smoking reefer. Danny didn't like her doing it. We groaned when she told us, and I thought then that I knew who it was that was doing all the screaming at night when they were having sex. *Shit,* I thought, *Theresa is whipped—Danny's putting it to her so good she can't even make her own decisions anymore.*

I'd been surprised when Nona hadn't put up a fuss about the smoking, but she told me later that she had already decided to cut back for the same reason—the baby.

"What you and Monique gonna name the baby?"

We both leaned back on the bench, the urgent need to get high satisfied, so we could relax and talk.

"Don't know yet. I'm trying to talk her out of some made-up shit she got from one of her sisters. It ain't right to name no child a name that ain't nobody heard of before and that ain't got no meaning."

My mind took off in two different ways, which was easy to do with some good reefer working in my system. First, I hadn't known that Monique had any people around, and second, Nona had made a deep-ass comment about the name shit. I was going to say something on one or the other topic, but I lost it as I noticed a leaf blow my way that was not entirely brown.

Nona cleared her throat, and I turned to her and stopped looking at the patterned leaf that had flipped over and over again.

"Pam, I got some troubles."

"Is it that little piss-ant Todd again? He been bothering you?"

"Nah, it ain't nothing like that. It's . . ."

She stopped, and I wondered if she too was taken in by the beauty of the night. How the clouds rolled in the sky, which was not the inky black of the usual midnights we had seen together. It was the difference between dark chocolate and milk chocolate—a variation, a shade—and I held my breath at the wonders that I could see in the projects with the reefer.

"We ain't never did nothing together."

"What you mean by that?"

"We ain't never got it on."

And then it was clear. Only I didn't know what to say. By then Nona had lit the other joint and she handed it to me; I was grateful to take a puff because for the life of me I didn't know how to respond. She had never fucked Monique?

"Okay, you gotta break this down for me, Nona. How the two of you get so hooked up if you ain't . . . ?"

"Don't know. I mean, I know but I don't know if I can tell you right. I just saw her and I knew. Just started by talking. And buying her things. That Todd, he wasn't in the picture, not really. And well, we kissed one day—that's about all 'cause she's always been pregnant. Ever since we met."

It was getting colder out, and I wanted to put my arms around my little sister and tell her to run from Monique. I wanted to tell her all that I had learned from Frank the clerk— if your heart has not been involved, leave. Because when you share stuff, when you have tasted them and they have tasted you, it is too late, and there will always be that feeling that makes you want to stay even when you need to be gone. If that's the way with men and women, that must be the way with all other lovers.

Screaming that she was crazy was out of the question too. I think she knew that already. Nona, the no-nonsense sister, the tough one, was hooked up with a woman and a baby on the way and had done nothing but kiss the girl and pledge, by her actions, to be there. Shit, she needed to run.

"I don't know what to tell you, Nona. Have you spoken to Monique?"

"Nah. I mean, I want to—you know—be with her, but now I think I gotta wait. The baby will be here soon, and it ain't a good idea to have all this sex just right yet."

I must have nodded. I was the middle sister, not the eldest, and my role had never been to tell anyone anything. I was not used to giving advice.

"Nona, you and Monique will work it out. It'll be all right."

She nodded and bowed her small head, and I wanted to hold her then and tell her about the world and how hard it was to make it by yourself and that she was asking for trouble with her black self trying to love another black woman-child with a baby on the way. Instead I took a long hit on the reefer and tried to forget what she had told me, forget about her troubles, because I couldn't do a damn thing for anyone.

When we walked back to the apartment, I put my arm around her neck, and she stayed that way for a few steps before she pulled away. That was all I could offer as comfort and all that she was willing to take.

SIXTEEN

We were all crowded in the examining room with Mama, watching the doctor make her cough while she listened to her lungs with the stethoscope and hit her knee with an odd-shaped hammer. It was early in the morning, and Theresa had made me and Nona go with them.

Even at seven-thirty the free clinic was full of people who were sick and poor and looked like there was something wrong with everything. While we were in the waiting room I wouldn't pick my head up. Sometimes I got sick to my stomach seeing people who were bandaged up with oozing sores and yellow pus showing through the gauze. I didn't want to see the way they wanted me to see. And people did want you to look at their sorrow. They'd first catch your eye, and if you made the mistake of even nodding, they had you. Then their eyes traveled to their sore area and they were telling you, *Hey, look at the pain I have here. Don't you feel sorry for me?*

Staring at the stained carpet, I decided that I would not make it as a nurse or a doctor. There was no way that I could have sick people stare at me and not be able to fix it so that they weren't sick anymore.

I wasn't mad at Theresa for making us come to the clinic,

but Nona was. She was still on a nod from the night before. She'd gone out late to get some air, smoke a joint, and play some ball. It was so crowded in the apartment, she'd told me one time, that she had to go out and stretch somewhere with no one around. But Baby Sister was still half high, and when we got into the cab I could see that her eyes were red and droopy.

"Y'all got to be able to take care of Mama in case something happen to me. We gonna go to the free clinic and I'll show you what to do."

The name of the place was really the Neighborhood Free Clinic, and a sick person had to sign up somehow—that part I wasn't sure about—but they could see the doctor for only five dollars. Maybe they never saw the same doctor twice and maybe they had to be there all day long, but it was still only five dollars, and that was a good deal for people who didn't have much more.

The nurse at the desk called Mama's name, and we all got up to go with her. Mama nodded at the lady.

"I was a nurse once too. Did you know that?"

"Yes, Mrs. Johnson. You've told us that before." The nurse was on the verge of rolling her eyes when she understood that there were three of us with Mama, and Nona didn't seem friendly in the least.

"Are these all your girls?"

"Yes they are, so you'd better cut the shitty attitude 'cause they don't like their mama treated bad."

Nona went to stand right behind Mama's elbow, and the nurse was quiet then and led us into the examination room.

"The doctor will be with you shortly."

We waited for a long time, not saying too much of anything to each other. Nona had finally given in and was sleeping, her head bent over and a soft whistle coming from her mouth.

Theresa sat with Mama and they flipped through an old *Jet* magazine that had been left in the waiting area.

"That James Brown, he sure do know how to keep that head combed. Wished I could get me a perm to do like his do."

"Mama, you look fine. You don't need no perm. You got an Afro now. You a real soul sister."

Mama put her fingers up to her Afro, which we had combed out right before the cab came for us.

"Really?"

"Mama, you look fine."

The door opened, and a large white woman came in holding a folder in her right hand and fumbling to put on glasses with her left. Her lab coat was so tight that the buttons were near bursting, and I wondered why she had it buttoned in the first place. Before saying anything she surveyed us and then glanced down at the chart, moving her lips silently. Nona woke up.

"Mrs. Johnson?"

"That's me, Doctor."

"My name is Dr. Renee Moore. I'm looking through your chart, and I see that you've been here a lot. Can you tell me what's wrong?"

My mother waited a couple of seconds, then looked at Nona, me, and Theresa.

"They say I done lost my mind."

"And what do you say?"

"That it's a matter of opinion."

I'd never heard Mama speak like this before. I jerked my head up.

"Why is it a matter of opinion?"

"Maybe I ain't lose it, maybe I just misplaces it every once in a while."

Mama gave the doctor one of the grins she gave to us when we brought her home a candy bar or a burger from McDonald's.

"Why would you want to misplace it?"

Mama shrugged, but there was a sly look in her eyes, and I didn't know what to make of how she was talking.

The doctor asked her to get on the examining table, and that's when she checked her heart, lungs, and reflexes.

"Everything's normal here. I'm going to ask you to disrobe. Ladies, I assume you are her daughters?" We all nodded.

"Okay, I need to see your mother alone for a while. If you don't mind, please go outside and have a seat."

Nona was ready to protest. I could tell she was mad. Having to get up so early in the morning only to be told that we couldn't stay with Mama didn't sit well with her. But Theresa nodded, so there was nothing else to be said. We followed her out to the waiting area.

We waited. And waited some more. About twenty minutes later, the nurse called us again to the room. Dr. Moore was standing when we entered, and Mama sat half naked on the examining table, dressed in a gown, the back open, the flesh of her back exposed. White scratch marks covered her arms from where she had raked her nails across her skin. I had told Theresa she needed better lotion to help her dry skin and to stop buying anything she saw on sale. I reached Mama first and tried to tie up the back of her gown.

The doctor was silent for a few moments.

"Theresa, Pamela, Nona, I've talked to your mother."

We were surprised that she used our first names.

"Are you familiar with the Good Book?" Nona and I turned to Theresa, but the doctor didn't wait for a response. "In that book, the Bible, it says that Jesus cast out demons. Do you remember that part?"

"Oh yeah, I do," chimed in Mama. "I remember that part good. Didn't he put that demon into some pigs and then send them over the cliff? Yeah, I remember that one."

"Good Geneva, very good." She spoke to Mama the way a parent does to a child.

That's when the doctor put down her chart and took off the glasses that had been hiding her eyes. As soon as I saw them, how they burned with an intense deepness, I called Kwai Chang, and he was there beside the doctor, staring over her shoulder at the chart on the desk.

"Pamela, I have been here for quite some time. I think you must remove your mother at once. The four of you are in danger." He nodded toward Mama. "Your mother will become sane and the three of you"—he nodded gravely in the direction of my sisters and me—"will be saved in the Christian manner."

The doctor was impatient. "I want all of you to gather in a circle. We're going to hold hands. First we're going to pray this demon away, and then we're going to give praise and thanks to the Lord for all He has done in your lives, all He will continue to do. Have any of you been saved?"

Her words ran from her mouth without her taking a breath. The glare of the light made her skin shine yellow. Her face was pointed upward as if to heaven. I noticed the heaviness of her jaw and how the meat fell from her cheeks and shook as she spoke. The frown lifted from her brow and she seemed excited—ready to help us, to save us if we weren't already. The eagerness to save reminded me of the open sores on the people in the waiting room, and I had trouble glancing in her direction.

Nona was the nearest to the doctor, and the woman laid a hand on Nona's head and began to chant. I didn't understand a word she was saying. Theresa sprang into action. She started dressing Mama swiftly, pulling her arms through her bra, throwing a sweater over her head. The problem came when she tried to fasten Mama's bra straps in the back. Mama's titties didn't take orders from nobody, especially not Theresa, who struggled to fit them into too small a bra. Kwai Chang turned his back away from Mama's nakedness. Nona stood unmoving, the doctor's hands glued to her scalp. I started to help Theresa and kept glancing at Nona as the doctor's voice rose.

"Girl, what you worried about? Gimme that sweater and my coat. When we goes out ain't nobody gonna be looking up under my coat. Now get me the hell outta here before she put them hands on me and I'ma hafta knock her down."

Without warning, Nona threw back her head and yelped. That's what I would call it, a yelp like a dog in heat, and it was such an astonishing sound that it stopped the doctor cold in her mumbling. Then Nona started to shake and twitch, her arms moving up and down, flapping like a giant bird. And with the flapping and yelping came the big feet marching. There was nothing but commotion in the room as the doctor struggled with Nona and we struggled to get Mama dressed. Kwai Chang stood apart even though there was barely room for a gnat with all of us crowded in the room and Nona marching and falling all over the place like a fool.

When we finished dressing Mama and got her up from the table, Theresa hustled her out, and I turned to Nona, who had slumped over the exam table that Mama had eased herself off of. The doctor was right there, hands firmly on Nona's head, pouring out words I didn't understand. I didn't know if Nona was fooling or not, but I did know that we had to get out of that office. I was trying to think of ways to move the doctor out of the way and snatch Nona.

Nona froze on the examining table. She went stiff with the exception of her right arm, which shot out and started moving wildly about, like she had no control.

"Oh Lord, come into this child. Claim this poverty-stricken soul. Show her what your love is like."

And I wanted to be like Nona, but worse. I wanted to thrash around and scream and holler. I bit my lip so hard that I felt the salt of blood on my tongue. I reached for Nona, trying to get her from the doctor's grasp.

"No, no, you have to leave her alone. Can't you see that she's feeling the Holy Spirit working in her? Let me finish praying."

All I knew was that I had to get Nona out of the room, away from this crazy woman. I moved so close to the woman that I could have kissed her. I smelled coffee on her lips.

"Let go of my sister." The voice did not belong to me or sound like me, but it was mine. The doctor was frightened. I could see it in the way she backed off, in the way she snatched her hand from Nona's head and moved toward the door with eyes that kept looking over the exam room. She didn't know what to do.

Nona sat up finally. Her eyes were just as red as they had been when we'd first gotten to the free clinic. When she got off the examining table, Nona pulled me behind her and stopped at the door, leaning in close to Dr. Moore. "Thank you for saving me," Nona said. "You did a good job."

Together we walked quickly past the nurses who framed the door. It took a moment for Nona's remark to sink in with the doctor.

"Don't come back here," she shouted. "You can't come back, ever. Not to a clinic in New York. I'll make sure. Your mama's not the only one crazy in your family."

I heard her but didn't turn back. I was drained—empty of even the desire to return her yells, to do anything other than get home. Kwai Chang had already faded away, an anxious frown on his face. His leaving felt bad to me, as if he judged our actions to be unworthy.

Nona and I caught up with Theresa and Mama outside and walked to the end of the block to hail a cab. Nona put her head on my shoulder and went to sleep. Mama giggled all the way home, telling us about how Jesus chased the demons and chased the money changers and all kinds of other things she now remembered about the Bible. I was glad to get back to our apartment and turn on the television and eat a bowl of Rice Krispies. It was only eleven o'clock, but it had been a long day.

SEVENTEEN

LATE ONE NIGHT THE MOANING SOUNDS FROM THE BEDROOM stopped me from sleeping. Mama's mouth was open, but she was on her stomach, her face pointed toward me. A thin line of drool was on the corner of her mouth, and while there was only a small amount of light from the table lamp I'd switched on, I could see that there was a wet spot on her pillow. And I saw her body as it moved with each snore, jerky, hard movements that shook the bed. The snoring and the moaning had me restless, and at first I lay there breathing deeply, trying to count or think of something else besides the sounds. Then I heard it—a low but long grunt, deep from the core of either Danny or Theresa, I didn't know which one.

When I rolled out of bed I was careful not to wake Mama. I'd have to get her water from the kitchen or even a cookie if her eyes opened. She'd stared at me before with disbelieving eyes, and I'd had to tell her that I was her mother and that I was only checking on her. That one had worked the best. She'd given me a sweet smile, an innocent one, and asked for the drink in a little squeaky voice. It made my heart stop and made me want to pee, I was so scared. She wasn't Mama then.

At first I told myself that I had to check to make sure that

Danny and Theresa were all right. The last sound might have meant there was trouble. Maybe he'd fallen from the bed or rolled on top of her by mistake and she was suffocating, and the only sound that she could make was that guttural one. And really she was calling for me: *Pam, Pam, come help me.*

I slid down the hallway, fingers touching the wall, feeling my way to the room. At the doorknob I hesitated, and before I could stop him I saw Kwai Chang. His face and body were plastered to the door like a poster print, and where I touched the knob it was icy cold. I could hear the moans now, muffled but increased in passion. They were panting together, I thought. I didn't know. But I wanted to see. I wanted to be in there so I could finally see which one of them was pouring their soul out into sex.

"You must not do this thing."

The whispered rush of words entered through my ears. I heard them. I understood. But I was compelled. The door had to open.

Scared, with sweat on my palms and fingers, I took the doorknob again. There was no glacial feeling. Kwai Chang had disappeared. I moved forward and made the door crack, then moved my head to peek.

The bedroom was small. It used to be Mama's. When we moved in we girls had taken the larger one. It was painted white, as were all of the other rooms in the apartment, but there was a different smell there—different maybe because it was Mama's by day and Danny and Theresa's by night. The room was lit with the fire of a dozen candles. I knew how many Theresa liked to use when Danny came around. The day before he'd spent the night the first time, I'd gone with her to the store. She'd chosen the reddest candles that she could find. An old Jamaican lady had told her that red candles meant passion and love. She'd put them around the bed, and on that first night she'd led him by the hand and he'd dropped his head to his chest, embarrassed because we all knew what was going to happen behind closed doors. Nona had chuckled and laid her head on Monique's lap, who cradled it and stroked her cheek. Mama had sat by the window and gazed outside, as there was nothing on television that appealed to her. I had sat alone too because I did not have anyone, not even Frank the clerk, on a regular basis.

So I looked inside the room. My eyes had to adjust, and I had to watch my breathing and the beating of my heart. I closed my eyes for one minute, maybe praying they wouldn't catch me, maybe hoping that they would.

He was sitting upright in the bed, propped up with pillows. His head was thrown back, and the sound was coming from his mouth, which was open and shaped in a perfect circle. He was like a man singing opera. Theresa was lying against his body, covering his massive stomach, and he was cradling her like a baby. I saw her hair and her naked body, and I was taking it all in because I didn't understand—until she shifted her body. Her mouth was glued to his nipple and her one free hand was working frantically to cup, to milk the large breast. She was tugging so hard that I believed she was trying to swallow him. He was not moving except for his head, but I believed he wanted to thrash and explode from pleasure, the way the sound kept coming from his mouth nonstop.

I moved, walking backward down the small corridor, but it was too late. Even if I'd wanted to, I couldn't take back what I'd seen. The greed in her movements as she suckled at his chest. That face of his, his mouth chiseled into a choirboy's O. I was ashamed. I felt hot and cold at the same time.

Mama was still asleep, but I knew that it would be a mistake to join her in bed. I'd toss and turn with the image and would wake her up. I dressed in the half darkness and quietly went out of the apartment. It was the only time I'd been out that late without Nona, but I wasn't afraid. There were too many people outside walking.

There was a girl pushing a baby carriage and a group of kids I knew from school who nodded in my direction as though they might not have minded me joining them on the benches. They were passing a joint between cupped fingers and laughing, not loud or boisterous laughter but the slow, low kind that comes with tiredness and winding down. I nodded to them also but moved on by myself. I was expecting Kwai Chang, and he did not disappoint me.

The eyes that he had for me were cold and distant.

"Why did you not respect them?"

"I know it was wrong," I said.

"It was very wrong."

We kept walking together on the streets, moving fast with an urgent pace. There were no words to share then, nothing that I could give to him to make him understand why I had done the forbidden. Sweat poured from my face, and when I looked up I was near my old house.

"Now do you understand the nature of men?"

He had asked me this question before—when I'd first had sex with Frank the clerk. I thought I'd known it then, but now I was positive that I had been wrong.

"What is the nature of a man?" I asked this on the corner of Ashford Street and Sutter Avenue, right in the middle of a streaming crowd of people who were coming out of the church. It was a late-night service, and I watched as people clutched their children close to them and their Bibles to their sides. They were afraid I was an addict, and I couldn't blame them. I had thrown on a pair of jeans shiny with ironed dirt and a T-shirt that had once belonged to flat-chested Nona. I had a baseball cap pushing my hair down so it looked like clown hair on the sides.

I was a miserable, pathetic Peeping Tom. Kwai Chang answered me with patience.

"It is the nature of a man to never be satisfied with what he has. We must always look, always seek, always know more than we need to know. Just like you tonight." He waited for me to digest this information.

"Although you are a woman-child, you are part of mankind and you have the same nature. Until you learn to be satisfied with what you have and understand what cannot be, you will be unhappy."

He bowed his head and turned away from me, and I became incensed.

"You goddamned mutherfucker. You phony. You fake. You dumb shit. Is that what you call wisdom? Or is that what you call fucking with my head?"

Someone touched my shoulder. I whirled, shaking it off.

"Sister, sister, who are you talking to?"

A crowd had gathered around me, closing in. I could smell the church now, only feet away from the open door. The furniture polish and waxed wood floor smell filled the air as the church folk surrounded me and began to lay hands on my head and hold my body.

"This is a prime example of our demon-filled youth. She is here spouting obscenities. Taking the Lord's name in vain. She's possessed. Can I get a witness?"

A few amens worked their way through the crowd, and I started to look for an opening. But the people pressed closer, and we were moving as a group into the church, one woman gripping one of my hands and half dragging me, a man in back of me so that I couldn't turn.

I started to scream. Not the pathetic scream of old horror movies when white girls get trapped and are waiting for Dracula. No, I screamed with my body, with my fists, and every other part of anything that moved. I knew that if I went through those doors, that if I let them examine my soul, I would not return. No more Pamela. So I fought.

"Child, why you struggling so hard? Don't fight Jesus. Come and join Him."

"You people ain't Jesus. So leave me the fuck alone." I tried to sit down so they would stop moving, but the old woman was strong—her callused hands held on like I was a snap bean from the field. There didn't seem to be any effort on her part at all to pick me up and keep me walking. I had a thought of how Mama, when she was in good health, had pushed, pulled, and carried us through temper tantrums. This woman had the same grasp of tempered steel.

All of them must have gotten the message when my right hand connected with the jaw of the woman dragging me and her Bible fell to the ground and her false teeth went flying in the street. They knew I was crazy then.

I broke free and ran all the way home. I stayed in the middle of the street most of the time, taking deep hurtful breaths and short pauses when I had to, cursing Kwai Chang, Theresa, Danny, and myself. And wanting things back the way they had been before I peeked.

EIGHTEEN

DADDY HAD BEEN ON MY MIND ALL DAY. THE THOUGHT OF HIM, the smell of him, the ghost of him hung around me like the lyrics of an old song that wouldn't stop playing in my mind. When I brushed my teeth in the morning I stared at my skin and thought that it was the same shade as his, deep and rich brown, and that I had hair that curled in all directions except for the right one, the one where it would lie down and behave. Theresa had his temperament, Nona had gotten his anger that could not be bottled once aroused, and I had inherited his features. Put us all together and you had Daddy. *Poor Mama,* I thought. No wonder she could never forget and go on with her life. Each time she glanced at us from the corner of her eye or heard us or maybe even sniffed us, there he was. I was sorry for the fact that I looked like him.

They had surprised me. It was my birthday, and I was seventeen. Theresa had splurged and gone to Mrs. Maxwell's to buy my cake, a quarter sheet, decorated with red roses and green stems. She'd beamed when they yelled "Surprise!" and I'd pretended to be happy seeing this kind of cake again in this family.

Every time someone had a birthday, Daddy would go to

Mrs. Maxwell's and bring back a sheet cake with buttercream icing—sweet, stomach-hurting icing that made me push hard on the toilet but which I couldn't resist. Passing the refrigerator, I'd open the box and stick a finger in it, or at midnight when we were supposed to be asleep, I'd cut a corner of the cake and stand at the door eating. Sometimes with the cake he produced a twenty-dollar bill and said to make sure we didn't spend it all in one place.

When he gave me money, I'd sweet-talk Theresa and she would take me to Times Square Stores, the last stop on the number 14 bus before it turned around and headed for Pitkin Avenue again. I'd head straight for the book department.

Now we didn't have Daddy. We had Danny, and he was cooking us a feast in honor of my birthday. We were having corn bread, fried catfish, collard greens, and macaroni with three different kinds of cheese melted in the pot. His big round face had a large grin, and he was happy, whistling in the kitchen and directing Theresa, who had chosen to help him since it was my birthday and I didn't have to do any work.

Mama was in the back room, silent. She'd been with us when they lit the candles on the cake and yelled, but she'd gone back to the other room when the present-giving started. There was a brief moment when I saw her expression as I opened the big red box from Nona, a gift set of a dictionary and thesaurus for college. Monique smiled when I kissed her too, and Mama shuffled off to her room, I supposed to watch television.

Danny came out to announce that the birthday girl's dinner was ready, and we set up the card tables. Theresa brought party hats and favors and we acted like little kids, blowing rude noises and making Danny frown because the food was getting cold.

When we were finally seated, Mama drifted from her room with her hands behind her back and stood next to me quietly until I finally gave her my full attention.

"I'm sorry I don't remember how old you is but I can tell you is about grown. You filling out them clothes pretty well."

Everyone laughed.

Her hand came from its hiding place and she put her gift to me on the table, in front of my plate. It was a framed picture of Daddy, young, dressed in an army uniform. He was handsome, with a neat mustache enveloping a toothy grin. I didn't remember ever seeing it before. The laughter had dried up, and before I knew it I was crying—not the deep crying that comes late in the night, but a couple of tears slid to my cheeks and my nose got stuffy.

Mama put a hand on my shoulder and squeezed it.

"Stop that there crying. We got us some food to eat."

She turned to Monique. "You over there, yeah, you with the big stomach. Go on in the kitchen and fix me a plate. Look like you need a little exercise. What's your name anyway?"

MY BIRTHDAY PARTY WAS OVER AND WE'D ALL SETTLED IN FOR the night when there was a faint noise at the door, as if someone was knocking but didn't want to be heard. It was the kind of knock that made me uneasy and giddy with hope. Since it was my birthday and I believed in miracles, I thought it might be Daddy using a hesitant tap, wondering if he would be welcomed or turned away. Kwai Chang appeared and nodded to me with a serious and intent face. For some reason he believed this to be an important visitor too.

I got to the door, Kwai Chang right behind me, moving with less urgency but on my tail anyway, and I didn't even look through the peephole. In the seconds that passed between the knock and my hand on the knob, I'd convinced myself that it was Daddy.

Her hand was poised to tap again, and she dropped it slowly when the door was flung open. It hadn't been too long ago that we'd nodded at each other on the elevator, or maybe it was at the park, but I didn't remember her being in such bad shape. Under her eyes were deep crescents like black quarter moons, swollen and throbbing. Her hair hadn't been combed in days and she needed a perm, her edges nappy and beading. When she talked I smelled the alcohol, Mad Dog 20/20.

"Thought you'd want to know—Frank is dead."

The words were in my head for an eternal moment before I understood.

"They figure somebody had a grudge or something. You know you can't be dealing around here without somebody getting hurt. Told him to stop the shit before he got in trouble but he ain't never listened to nobody. Not even when we was growing up."

We stood in the doorway while she told me about Frank, and I thought that maybe I should ask her to come in, but I didn't want her to stop talking.

She was different from when I'd first met her. Now she was slumped and disheveled. More like a trick bitch from the corner than the mean fighting woman I had come to think of her as.

"I don't want to hold you or nothing. I thought I'd better tell you because he would have wanted you to know."

It was difficult for me to do more than slide my eyes across her face, but there was gratitude in my heart even as it was squeezed tight with the knowledge that Frank the clerk was dead.

"But who are you? What's your name? How did you know Frank?"

She stopped and turned around, and I saw a glimpse of a smile.

"It ain't important what my name is. Me and Frank, we used to be a thing. I had his first baby."

She saw my shock and chuckled.

"Back in those days I was littler than you is. Girl, I was fly, little everywhere except for my tits and ass. Had all the men going crazy for me. But all I wanted was black-assed Frank. I ain't loved no man like I loved him."

"But what happened? You didn't stay together?"

"Girl, I grew up. And as much as I was crazy for him, he ain't feel the same for me. He kept leaving and coming back. He'd get with somebody and come back to me when they was finished. I couldn't take it." She paused, and her mouth became gentle.

"Remember this for when you get a man of your own— don't let him do that. Make him choose. Can't be in and out of your bed. It ain't no good." She seemed to be searching her mind to tell me more important things. I could see the vein moving on her forehead, and I knew her sadness was worse than the one I carried around. So I waited.

"We got closer when I told him we couldn't do it no more. A woman gotta set up some rules. Then he started loving me like I was important to him—like we was brother and sister. He told me all about you and your quiet self."

She turned again to leave, and I wanted to reach out and put my hand on her, to give her some type of touch that would show that I'd loved him too. And it was hard for her to go because she turned around again to speak.

"I think he loved you best of all. It tore him up when you said you wouldn't meet him no more. He was picked up a few days later. Too damned sloppy after that. Couldn't concentrate."

I was glad Kwai Chang was there, next to me, keeping me strong.

She walked down the gray hallway and to the elevator, and I wondered if I ever would be the same again. My poor beautiful black Frank the clerk. Gone.

This was all too much heartache for me, too much for the

day, too much to happen in one lifetime that passed for twenty-four hours. I broke into my emergency stash, rolled a joint, and closed the bathroom door.

LIKE A SICK JOKE MY PERIOD FLOODED ME THE MORNING AFTER I learned about Frank. I told Theresa that I was having cramps and crawled back into the unmade bed. Before leaving, she came to sit on the bed and made me take some water with an aspirin. She felt my head and kissed me on the cheek like she was a sane Mama, and all I wanted to do was hit her or take the live hand that caressed me and bite to the bone. When she left, I took four more aspirin and slept the whole day.

NINETEEN

NONA DECIDED THAT SHE SHOULD GIVE MONIQUE A REAL BABY shower. She gave Danny fifty dollars to buy the food and me and Theresa twenty dollars to buy a present for the baby and decorate the apartment.

"Is that gonna be enough?" Nona asked as she paced back and forth, fingers stuffed in her pockets, unable to remain still.

"More than enough," lied Theresa.

"Good, good. I'm gonna order a cake from Mrs. Maxwell's. I only got forty left."

"Nona, you sure you wanna spend so much for this? When the baby come y'all might need it."

Nona stopped walking.

"Baby gotta be welcomed right. I'll pick up some extra hours at the car wash on weekends. Maybe even go over to the fish place with you and Danny. I know I got to be ready when the baby gets here. I plan on being ready." I wanted to ask what Monique was going to do while Nona worked so hard, but I couldn't find it in me to make my sister feel bad about trying to do good.

"Don't need all of this here to buy food for one dinner."

Danny gave her back twenty dollars. Nona was ready to hand it back but she stopped, nodded, and left the room.

We decorated the apartment with pink, white, and blue balloons and paper streamers we got at the dollar store. Danny was making spaghetti with sausage instead of beef. And he had some Italian bread with real butter and salad. I watched him a few minutes while he threw spices into a simmering pan of meat with onions and sauce. He shook a small fistful of salt and pepper mixed together and sprinkled it a little at a time over the pan. Then he put in oregano and small pieces of garlic he had chopped up on a plate. I wanted to ask him about the cooking, have him talk to me, but he was too involved. Sometimes he was like that—too into his own world to answer. So I left him turning around and around on swollen ankles in a kitchen that was too small to fit him. But he was okay, loving the cooking more than he hated the smallness of the space.

When Nona brought Monique in from wherever they had been, we all yelled, "Surprise!" Monique had to sit down, and her eyes watered with starry tears as she clutched her belly.

"I didn't think I was gonna get no baby shower."

"Well, you was wrong," said Nona, her chest puffed up like a strutting rooster.

We pulled chairs into the living room, got paper plates, and ate until we couldn't move. Mama had three helpings and walked around holding her stomach.

After we rested, Monique wanted to dance. We turned the radio on to WBLS, and Frankie Crocker started rocking some tunes. Since none of us really knew what we were doing, Monique had to take charge and teach us how to do the Bus Stop, and she went on to show us the Hustle. Danny was sitting in a chair, leaning back and smiling. Theresa was at his feet, one hand on his knee. Monique had Mama as a partner, trying to teach her some steps, and me and Nona was swinging each other around by the arms and falling all over everyone.

We didn't stop until midnight, and that was only because the people in the apartment downstairs started knocking on their ceiling. So we cleaned up and started for bed. In the hallway I saw Monique grab Nona by the waist and plant a kiss on her lips, one of those long, lingering kisses that you see in the movies between Humphrey Bogart and Ingrid Bergman.

I was a little embarrassed watching, but I figured that now I knew for sure that they were dykes, having proof with my own eyes.

"Hey, y'all cut that shit out. Go get a room." Theresa walked by and hit them with a newspaper, and they broke apart giggling. *Not a bad day,* I thought, *not bad at all.*

TWENTY

Monday was not good. I overslept and missed first-period English. My guidance counselor pulled me into his office, his fingers pressing into my flesh, and I thought that it might have been the first time that a white person had touched me on purpose. They hadn't been a part of my life. I'd noticed them at school, of course—they were my teachers, and there were even some fellow students that I laughed with—but I hadn't allowed any touching. Now he had his hands on me, and he pushed me gently into a seat opposite him.

"Now, tell me what is going on with you. I had you on track as going to college next year, but you're cutting classes. Too many classes. If you don't stop, you won't be able to graduate."

He wasn't a big man. I would have classified him as tiny. He had an eagle beak nose and a skinny body that needed to eat some food cooked by Danny.

I saw this man often in an informal way. He was a runner. If I happened to get into school early, he'd be on the track, slowly running around and around. I thought of him as a sack of bones with a mission: to make it around and back as many times as he could.

I wanted to tell him, since I hadn't told anyone else, that it was hard for me to sleep at night, hard for me to get up in the mornings, hard for me to breathe with any type of regular rhythm in my chest since Frank died. He'd been in lockup, but that didn't mean that it didn't hurt not to have him on my side. I wouldn't ever be able to touch him again or feel the hunger in his arms when he was holding me as tight as he must have held the other, nameless woman when he was loving her. I was such a confused, mixed-up jumble of feelings that I was only able to smile and assure him that I would make it to class.

"You know, if you're having difficulty, maybe you'd like to talk. If not to me, then to someone else."

He hadn't said anything like this to me in the three years I'd been at the school. I wondered if everyone could tell how close I was to exploding, if my other teachers had gotten together and said, *Hey, you, guidance counselor, you go in there and sit her down and find out what the hell is wrong with her. Why is she being a problem now when she has never been a problem before?*

I figured his skinny self had finally bowed under the weight of their demands, and so he'd approached and used the I-care-and-I-give-a-damn look on me. He hadn't drawn back when he touched me. But even though these thoughts spewed hotly in my brain, I didn't allow him to see or feel any of it. Just like I hadn't told anyone about Frank or how crazy my mother really was.

Instead, I nodded my reassurances, stood, and walked swiftly from the room. I knew he would never understand more because I didn't think I could tell my story the way it should be told. Nobody would have believed any of the shit anyway, and even if they had, what could they possibly have done? Take Mama to the hospital and split us all up? Make Frank live again? Bring back Daddy? Make me care about getting up every day?

When I got home, Theresa was leaving with Nona and Monique for the free clinic. Monique was eight months pregnant, and the baby would be here anytime. She told me to keep an ear out for Danny because he was coming by the house.

To pass the time and not think about school I asked Mama if she wanted me to scratch her head.

"Scratch it?" she asked while putting a tentative finger near her front edges.

"Yup. Remember how I used to do it?"

She shook her head.

"Just hold on."

I went into the bathroom and got a wide-toothed comb. When she sat down I spread a towel around her neck and began to undo her plaits. Mama's hair was wiry, so tough in some places that you could cut your hand. But I took my time, parting it and scratching out the dandruff and putting a dab of Dixie Peach to the scalp. She was asleep with her head tilted forward in about five minutes, and I had to smile at her snores—the way she had of using both her mouth and her nose and making it sound like snorting instead of snoring. Mama was funny even when she was asleep.

I heard Danny's step outside before he knocked and I whipped the door open, expecting to help him with grocery bags. But he was empty-handed, standing in front of me with a torn shirt ripped from his waistband and blood trickling from a split and torn lip. He staggered into me, and I nearly fell from his weight but was able to hold on because the wall was behind me. I stepped back, all the while trying to leverage his body.

The door closed, and within seconds I felt the pressure of his body ease. I found myself eye to eye with Mama, whose hair was standing on end, a comb hanging from the side of her head.

"Come on," she said, "let's get him to the couch." And we did manage to move him, coaxing slow footstep after slow footstep from him until we could help him bend his knees to sit.

"Boy, what happened to you?" Her eyes were alert, taking in everything, her hands patting his arms to give him comfort.

"Go get him some water, Pammy. And bring back some ice while you're at it."

I stood by Mama for a second, confused. Here she was giving me orders in her old voice and there was Danny sitting on the sofa, disoriented. Something was wrong, but I didn't have enough time or understanding to put it all together before Mama grabbed the towel from around her neck and used it to swat me out of the room.

"Go on now. The boy needs help."

When I got back she had taken off his shirt. There were nasty bruises where his ribs were swallowed by fat. He was hairless, as smooth as a newborn baby, and I could see where Theresa might delight in running her hands over such soft-looking skin.

Mama snatched the ice from me and pressed it against his lip. Danny moaned, and it was the first sound that I had heard from him other than the groan of the couch as he sat. He let Mama doctor on him and was silent as she cleaned him up.

"I asked you what happened earlier. You ain't said nuthin'."

This was the Mama I remembered—the Mama from the house before the projects, who knew how to handle things like beaten-up men.

"I was coming over to cook, had some bell peppers, chopped meat, and white rice. These guys stopped me and before I could do anything, they had me on the ground. I wasn't expecting it, that's all. They didn't hurt me too bad."

Danny was far off from us, maybe dazed, maybe reliving getting the shit kicked out of him. But he was hurt, and anybody with two eyes could see it wasn't from the torn-up lip or purple bruises.

"We gotta call the police," Mama said. She headed for the telephone.

"Nah. Police ain't gonna do nothin' 'cause I didn't see no faces."

There was a silent moment that ended when Danny tried to stand.

"I gotta get myself together. I can't let Theresa see me like this." It was as if he was trying to shake off bad luck, the way he tipped his shoulders back and shook himself before he moved on. He took a couple of deep breaths, picked up his torn shirt, and went to the bathroom in the back. Mama and I sat shaking our heads at each other, not talking with words because we didn't need to. *It is a shame,* we said. *What is this world coming to? Can't even have company.*

He came back into the living room, and I saw that his eyes were more focused but he still wasn't Danny yet. A beat-down was something you had to recover from, especially when you hadn't ever had one before.

"It just surprised me. I been walking these streets all my life and I ain't never got jacked like this. I ain't seen it coming." He said *surprised,* but it was more than that. I think he was hurt. He was a big guy; people knew him. If they didn't respect him, they respected his size. And to be attacked when it was still light out, where people could see . . . It was more than the food and the money they took from him, it was all about respect.

"I don't think I'm gonna stay. I need to change my shirt and stuff. I need to go home."

No matter that Mama and me begged him to rest, to at least go over to Brookdale or wait for Theresa, he wouldn't budge. As he ducked out the door, he asked us not to tell anybody about his being jacked. We could say that he hadn't shown up. He made us promise by saying that if we kept his secret he'd make us a pound cake when he came back around.

When he left there was no relief in my stomach, and I kept picturing his big body rolled over in some ditch. I should have asked him to call as soon as he got home, but I hadn't thought of it. Since there was nuthin' either of us could do, I went back to scratching and greasing Mama's head and yelling out the questions to the *Jeopardy* answers she repeated over and over—that was how she handled things when she was scared or nervous.

Theresa, Nona, and Monique got in late. I had already put Mama in the shower and fed her some leftovers from Danny's last visit. When I saw Theresa's face I knew something was wrong. Her lips were drawn together and she moved slowly with a jerky gait, almost as if she had forgotten how to walk. I watched her sit and Monique sink down heavily beside her on the love seat. Theresa moved and put her hand on the girl's belly, rubbing it gently. Nona tensed, her long muscular arms flexed because of the fists at her side.

"Did anything happen to Danny today?" Theresa stared at me and I was afraid.

"Yeah." The answer came from Mama, who had slipped in from her bedroom, standing at the door. "They beat his ass and we had to fix him up. Why?"

"Goddamn mutherfucker." Nona turned and punched the concrete wall so hard that she doubled up in pain, but then she lashed out with her foot, kicking so hard she made a small dent.

"Stop it, Nona. Just stop it. What you think, we got money to pay for some hole in the wall?" Mama tightened her bathrobe, and it was sense that was coming from her lips again. We all turned in surprise.

"Okay, Theresa, why you asking 'bout that boy of yours?"

"Monique's ex. He stopped us. Told us he had got a hold of Danny. He thought Danny was taking care of Monique. Didn't believe Monique and Nona was together. Said he was gonna kill Danny if he didn't let Monique go."

"He ain't gonna do nuthin'. I'ma kick his ass. I'ma kill him if he get close to my family again."

"You!" Mama moved closer to Nona, grabbed her arm, and whirled her around until they were facing one another, eyes locked with hardness and anger.

"You ain't doing nuthin'. We getting ready to get outta this place. We ain't living here no more. We can't have people beating up our friends coming to cook for us and we ain't having nobody mess with that child over there or the baby we gonna have."

Theresa sucked in a breath, and Nona slumped next to Mama and put her head on her breast and let Mama stroke it without a murmur. I don't know whether it was tears or sweat that coated her face. Monique's head was down. Her long fingers splayed across her belly, Theresa gripping one of her pinky fingers, giving our new little sister comfort.

"You think I don't know? You think I'm so crazy that I don't know that your girl over there? That the fat boy what come over here to cook belong to Theresa—to us too? We getting ready to go. Y'all start packing up our stuff. Tomorrow we going over to the rent office and tell them and ask for us a new place, somewhere else. We ain't staying here for my people to get hurt."

She took Nona's head from her breast and held it for a moment before kissing her forehead and cheeks.

"You is mine. You came from me. I'ma take care of you until I can't do it no more. I promise."

From across the room there was a small gasp. Monique looked at Theresa, wide-eyed with surprise and embarrassment.

"I just wet my panties."

TWENTY-ONE

MAMA GOT HER MIND TOGETHER LONG ENOUGH TO PRETEND to be Monique's mama, and that got her into the delivery room. Monique hollering loudly for Nona got *her* in. I was glad not to be anywhere close because I did not want to see anything.

Danny and Theresa and me sat together in the lounge. I couldn't really look at them—the image of his tit in Theresa's mouth kept intruding when all I wanted to do was make a decent conversation. So I was quiet and waited until Nona came out. Since Theresa and I knew her, we knew she was just about to throw up—which made me feel even better about not being in that room with Monique screaming like she was a nut or an addict kicking the habit.

"She okay now and we got us another girl in the family."

I watched as Nona swallowed down whatever it was that she had been going to throw up. As her shoulders untensed she started to smile and act like she was proud. Danny stood up and went over to her and offered his hand like they were men together. And I could see that Nona liked that. She gripped him strongly back. Then she did something I'm not sure I've ever seen her do before. She moved up closer on Danny and hugged him. Then she kissed him, and I swear I almost fainted on the spot.

When Nona left to go back in with Monique and Mama, Danny stood there in the same spot for a minute. He reached his fat hands to his cheek and touched the spot that Nona had kissed. Then he turned to me and Theresa and smiled. He was so like the picture of Buddha that I'd seen in my history textbook that I was going to say something, but I stopped myself. Sometimes you can just be quiet.

He and Theresa held hands until Mama and Nona came out again and we all took a taxi home.

TWENTY-TWO

On the day Monique was due back from the hospital, Danny was up at dawn fixing food. We were going to have a turkey, a ham, potato salad, collard greens, macaroni and cheese, black-eyed peas, corn bread, and a few sweet potato pies. He'd also picked up some fresh cucumbers and tomatoes for a salad if Monique didn't want to eat as heavily as the rest of us. All the while he talked to me he was singing and doing little dances across the kitchen floor. Theresa grinned at him each time they passed each other and somehow managed to touch him or kiss him. Mama was back to her old normal crazy self and put on the Five Blind Boys and started to dance.

Even as I smiled, the thought of Frank swirled inside me, and I could almost taste him in the back of my throat, where the tears were gathered but afraid to come out.

Theresa went with Nona to pick Monique and the baby up from the hospital, and Danny went downstairs at about the time he thought they were getting back. We never knew when the elevator might go on the blink, and he wanted to be able to carry the baby upstairs if they needed help.

I was glad for the time alone. I stirred the greens and made

Mama change her clothes because she had perspired through her housedress from dancing so hard. She smiled.

"The baby's coming, ain't she?"

"Yep. She gonna be here soon."

"Is they gonna let me hold her? I did at the hospital, you know."

"Mama, of course you gonna hold her. We all gonna hold the baby."

She stood at the door to the kitchen, watching me take care of the food.

"Go on now, Mama. You got to get changed from those clothes."

She still didn't move, and I turned to her.

"Pammy, you is a good child." She smiled and went down the hall singing.

IT SEEMED AS THOUGH WE ATE FOR DAYS AFTER WE PASSED THE baby around. Mama held her first. Monique told us her name was Pure Joy. I glanced in Nona's direction, and all she gave me was a proud grin. Pure Joy was all right by her. We gathered around the sofa and waited our turn to hold her. Monique finally took our new queen and laid her down in the middle of the bed. And then we ate and ate and ate.

Later I slipped away from them all. I had not invited him in some time, not in my head or in my presence, but now I called him, and he was at the foot of the bed, standing near me, looking at me look at the baby.

"Isn't she beautiful?" I asked as I moved around to sit on the bed next to her. I lifted the blanket away from her feet and touched her toes and then her little fingers. The baby stretched and yawned as I leaned forward, wanting to breathe her smell. The air around her trembled, shimmering like a waterfall or a fire.

"Yes, she is beautiful."

And we said nothing more to each other. We smiled, and I stroked the baby, who could have been mine and Frank's. Kwai Chang quietly stood at a distance with grace and a half smile on his full lips.

There was a loud bang from the front of the apartment, then another. The baby kicked out a thin foot, and I quickly gathered her to me. There were screams.

I was holding the baby tight to me as I moved down the hallway. I heard Danny.

"Man, you need to put that gun down. You don't wanna hurt nobody."

"You shut the fuck up. This ain't none of your business. This between Monique an' me."

"Todd, Todd, please put the gun down. I'll go with you. Just don't hurt nobody here." Monique was crying. I could hear it in her voice. Tears were dripping down her face, and her mouth was full of them.

"Ain't nobody going no place." That was Nona, strong and brash. I was scared, holding on to the baby, and started moving back to the room slowly.

There was a shot, then another and another, and I didn't know who was screaming louder, me or Theresa.

Without knowing how I'd gotten there, I was in the bedroom, and I had enough sense to take the baby and slide her under the bed with a prayer. Kwai Chang had his fingers on his mouth and was gesturing for me to get under the bed with our baby, but I ignored him.

I went into the living room and saw Theresa on the floor, rocking and moaning, with Danny's head in her lap and bright red, red blood streaming from his big stomach. His hand was on her face and she was kissing it.

Todd was on the floor too, with his eyes wide open and his

body trembling. And last there was Mama, almost on top of him, her head near the waist of his sweat pants, her hands gripped around his wrist, the gun a finger's length away from them both on the floor.

"Mama," I was hollering. "Mama, Mama."

THE NEIGHBORS CAME AND THEN THE POLICE CAME. IT WAS crowded and then empty as they took us someplace for the night. There was no quieting Theresa, but she was not loud, only constant.

"Danny, Mama, Mama, Danny."

Nona and Monique had the baby, and every time Nona was about to break, each time I saw tears ready to fall, Monique pushed the baby on her and Nona bent down and wiped her tears on the blanket.

I couldn't move. My feet, legs, arms and even my mouth were tired, sore. I sat by myself, rocking with each moan from Theresa.

WE WERE MOVING AGAIN, LIKE SOME FAMILY ADRIFT, SET APART from others and yet the same too because of our lack of men. Mama was gone; the old Danny had died; Theresa was silent. Nona and Monique held their treasure near us, and we took turns being happy with her in our laps. That was all we had for the time being, but I kept searching. I was sure he must have seen, must have heard that she was gone. That we needed him. And I was waiting for the knock on the door, for the forgiveness pain that would encircle our family and make it halfway whole again. *Daddy, I cry in my pillow at night, why don't you come to us?*

Oh, fuck him. Fuck the day he made me, fuck the day he became a daddy. He doesn't deserve to be loved. I was rocking on the floor in the middle of the night. There was a pillow jammed against my mouth, and if I'd taken it away I would have woken the whole building up with my screams.

In a few minutes it was over, and the fury that had made me angry instead made me so tired that I crawled to the bed. When I slipped my feet into the bed it was cold and I was not comforted. No Mama. No warmth.

TWENTY-THREE

DANNY DIED THAT DAY AND THEN HE CAME BACK TO LIFE. AND all the grief we had sitting in our stomachs for Mama had to wait because we were too busy trying to make sure that Danny did not die and leave us like everybody else had.

Theresa and me took turns sitting by his bed and holding his hand and talking to him. Nona couldn't do as much because she was helping Monique with our baby, who didn't seem to know the difference between night and day. Pure Joy hollered when the sun went down and breathed hard and deep at the first signs of light.

Other people would've said that she was confused and needed to be put right, maybe even put on a schedule. But we talked about it and said amongst ourselves that she was the smartest baby alive and if there was some reason she wanted to scream and play and kick in the nighttime, so be it. We would wait until she decided to turn things around.

Danny's mother came to see him once. She was a thin, stooped-over lady with bad breath and watery eyes. She went to him and stroked his arm and cried a small tear that she wiped with a swollen finger. She asked which one of us was Theresa.

"I ain't able to get around much so I'm glad you gonna be able to be here and take care of him. He can go home with you when they let him out. I just ain't able to care for him."

Even though Danny wasn't able to talk, since they had a respirator over his mouth and nose, he understood what she said. He turned his head away from her as she hobbled out of the room. I slipped my hand back into his, squeezing so he would look in my direction.

"Dontcha worry none about her. You is our family now," I heard Theresa say, and I nodded. I thought I saw him smile, but it was hard to tell with that plastic mask on. When he squeezed my hand I knew for sure that he was going to be okay with being with us and giving up his mama, who didn't seem to want him in the first place. It was a good feeling to know that he loved us too.

But Danny changed. And I always think that the old Danny really did pass on that operating table when they were trying to get the bullets out of his belly. Despite the fact that Mama had done her best to save him, the spirit and heart of Danny passed on that day, and we all knew it for sure when they let him out of the hospital.

First he took no joy in eating, and then he found no joy in cooking. He got littler and littler. The doctors had to take out most of his stomach and part of one of his intestines, I don't know which, but it made eating hard for him. Sometimes he would stand in front of the stove, fat, greasy sausages cooking and smelling up the whole apartment, and he would start to cry.

"I ain't got no urges no more. I don't want nuthin'. No cornbread, no meat, no chocolate cake." He'd shake his head and go to the living room to sit down, leaving me or Monique to finish the cooking as best we could.

Danny got to be skinny right before our eyes. His face got cheekbones and his eyes no longer resembled a Buddha's, squinting between folds of fat. He had a waist and a smaller behind. Theresa went out and bought him some jeans and a belt to hold them up in case she was wrong about the size. They were supposed to cheer him up, but when he saw them he only started crying again and left the room, heaving out his sorrows in the air because he could not tell us exactly what was wrong.

But we kept on trying, talking to him and making him a part of our family. And one night, when I heard the high-pitched singing from the room again, I knew that things were getting better. The old eating Danny was gone. Dead. And we had to get used to the new one. But at least we had a Danny. That was the good thing.

WE HAD MAMA'S FUNERAL ON A THURSDAY, AND IT WAS preached by a man Mama had never met and who couldn't pronounce her name. Every time he went to say it, it came out *Gene-via* instead of *Geneva*. Nona was ready to get up and fight him—I could feel it in the way her shoulder tensed up against mine. But Aunt Pinky was there, and she held Nona down. I never thought I'd be glad to see the Zombie Sisters again, but Pinky did save the preacher from a sure butt-kicking that day.

Aurora and Zora were quiet until the part where the family has to say good-bye. That's where they make you walk around and stare at the body and sometimes people touch the coldness that is left. Aurora shouted first, and then Zora followed. They were ready to knock the flowers over, and for sure I thought I saw Zora trying to climb in the coffin. But it was too much effort to lift her legs, and she settled for keening and crying so hard it would have made you think Mama was her baby. The way they acted made me think of me and Nona in the doctor's office.

Pinky took a moment and looked around the funeral parlor. There was no one there but our small family of women. She went up front. I thought she was going to put her arms around her sisters and try and pull them from the coffin. But she didn't.

She stepped back, lifted her arm, and slapped the piss out of Aurora. It was a loud stinging slap that stopped the organist cold.

"Pull it together, stupid."

When we got outside, Pinky lit a cigarette and inhaled deeply. The funeral director was frowning at her for smoking, but Pinky didn't care. She looked him up and down like she might be inclined to hit him too. Just then I saw Nona in her. Nona was a younger version of Pinky.

"I'm sorry about that in there. We didn't mean to come here and make no trouble." Pinky spoke as little curls of smoke drifted our way. "We sorry about your mama too. I know it didn't seem like it but we loved her." Pinky shrugged. "We just couldn't see her like she was. Didn't think we wouldn't have time to make it right."

She threw her cigarette down on the steps and ground it out with a pointy-toed shoe. The funeral man followed her movements. She looked up and smiled at him. Then she turned to us.

"We leaving now, but we'll be around."

There was no hugging or kissing or tears. We watched the three of them walk off and I knew they would be coming back. What I didn't know was how I felt about them being in our life again. Behind us the preacher gently coughed, and that was our signal to pay him for the service.

"Can we get half price because you ain't said her name right, not even one time?" Nona stared the preacher full in the face, and that was the only time I felt like laughing the whole day.

TWENTY-FOUR

THE GUIDANCE COUNSELOR PULLED ME INTO HIS OFFICE AGAIN, only this time it was with a gentle touch, a mouth that was not as stern, and eyes that tried to tell me how much he cared.

"Well, Pamela, I know this has been a horrible year for you, with the tragedy and all. . . ."

He was, I think, the type of person who could express sympathy easily. Most people hadn't been able to say those things. They left me alone, and I was glad for their fear because mine was even greater—I didn't want to let anyone see me cry.

"But I did want to let you know that you will graduate with your class."

There was an expectant pause, and he waited for me to smile or show some type of interest but it was difficult for me to do more than nod. He cleared his throat.

"And, ah, the principal was able to pull some strings. We think you'll be able to start school at the junior college this summer. You'll have to fill out the application, of course, make sure everything's in on time, but you'll be able to start if you want."

The "if you want" was said so that I'd know how stupid it would be of me not to want it. But I wasn't stupid. I wanted to go to college. For a second I pictured the coming fall, and the thought of walking down another hallway burdened with books and schedules made me forget that I had not been happy in a long time.

"Thank you," I said what I thought Danny would have said, and I got up to leave.

"If you ever need anyone to talk to . . ."

"Thank you," I said again, because I didn't know what else might be appropriate. There was an awkward parting. The last thing I remembered about him was his beak nose and his disappointment that I wouldn't speak to him or cry on his shoulder.

TWENTY-FIVE

ON GRADUATION DAY I SAT WITHOUT FIDGETING WHILE
Monique straightened my hair, careful of the knotty kitchens in
the back and in my edges. Curling smoke drifted from the eye
on the stove, and Monique's face dripped sweat. She held up a
parted section of hair and started the comb at the root, careful
not to touch the scalp. I was perfectly still, not wanting her to
burn me. Each time she picked up the hot comb, she blew on it
and waved it around for a couple of seconds and pressed it on
the clean dish cloth she had ready near the stove.

"You ever thought about getting a perm? I think your hair
could take it real well."

We hadn't been talking, and hearing her voice startled me.
I don't know where I was, just drifting on thoughts, imagining
something somewhere and wishing she would finish soon.

"Excuse me?"

"I think you should get a perm. Then you wouldn't have to
go through this hair frying all the time." There was a short
pause. "Fixing hair. That's what I want to do."

"If you really want to do it, then you will."

"How you so sure of everything? How you get to be like
that? I ain't sure of nothing."

She had a tremor in her voice, and she might have been close to crying. But the hands that held the straightening comb were steady, and I decided to have faith and not flinch. She continued to work quietly, parting my hair with a wide-toothed comb and working the heat through my roots so that I would finally look like all the other black girls graduating that day. I didn't know whether it was a good thing or not. I had never looked like them before, but here I was on graduation day— I'd look like them and have fried hair to smell like them too. When she finished straightening my hair, she pulled two pairs of curling irons out of a small paper bag and sat them on the hot eyes of the stove.

"Now you can't fall asleep while I'm curling you. We gotta be careful so you don't get burnt." Her voice was firm, but as soon as she said that my head started to nod. My eyelids fluttered. I wanted a nap.

"Now you better stay awake or you gonna go to your graduation with a big old burn mark on your head. Stay awake, Pammy."

That caught me off guard—her calling me Pammy.

"Don't call me that." Listening to myself, I thought I sounded harsh, like Nona could sound when she was hurt. But Monique kept working on my head, softer now, gentler. Her touch was feather light on my scalp, and I had the feeling that she did not want to intrude more or disturb my thoughts.

I stayed awake because she had robbed me of the desire to sleep. Now every second was full of Mama and Frank.

Strange that I thought so little of Daddy, especially today. My other losses tallied up to more. I knew there was a future with thoughts of him again, looming. The two I'd lost couldn't come back, but Daddy could. That was the difference.

Monique was finished.

"You want me to comb you out?"

More than a question, it was a plea. She should have said, *I didn't mean to call you Pammy. I know only your mother called you that. It'll never happen again. I'm gonna keep my place.* When I didn't answer she started again.

"I want to beg your pardon."

"Huh?"

"It was my fault that Todd came up here like he did. He was chasin' after me and the baby. It's my fault your mama gone like she is and I'm so sorry."

I heard her put the curling iron on the stove. Then I heard the crying that sounded as if it was being pulled from her chest, racking sobs that would not stop. I could picture the slobber and spittle and snot that was all over her face, because crying sounds like that do not leave a pretty picture.

There was a fear in me that if I got up and turned around and saw her crying, I'd start and not be able to stop. I could feel the tears climbing from deep in the pit of my stomach. But there was more than my tears that wanted to fly out of me, and I refused to touch that place deep down to see what else would come up.

Theresa walked in. She was holding the baby, who by then was content to have any one of us hold her at any time. And that was what Monique needed. Theresa waited while Monique wiped her hands on the front of her shirt and took the baby, holding her tight. I was finally able to look in her direction, but it took me a minute or two and several deep breaths to say, "Thank you for doing my hair. I appreciate it."

TWENTY-SIX

I HAD A NEW DRESS IN THE CLOSET THAT THERESA AND NONA had bought for me. It wasn't from Pitkin Avenue. We'd gone to A&S on Fulton Street and picked it out of the Young Miss department, where the gray-haired white ladies followed us around instead of the Puerto Ricans. Theresa said that we had gone big time, seeing as how we had a different class of people suggesting we were shoplifters. Nona didn't think it was funny and neither did I.

It was a beautiful dress, pure white with little bell sleeves and a large white ribbon folding around my waist. When Monique finished, I went to my room and dressed. I was all right up until I looked in the mirror and thought about them again. It was shitty to be caught in an endless cycle of tears.

I tried to comb my hair, but each time I lifted one arm, the other became too weary to bear. Finally I had to sit still and breathe, all the while telling myself that it was no use to think of the dead because I had the living.

There was heat and a shimmering feeling in the room. The air was shaking in front of my eyes. I went to turn on the fan, and when I paused in front of the mirror again, there he was, without introduction, without my having asked for him to come. He ducked his head in his manner and began to speak to me.

"You are well this morning?"

"Yes," I said. "I'm fine."

"It is an important day for you, isn't it? I am glad that you are graduating, going on your journey." We nodded at each other, and there was an awkwardness that had never been there before.

"I have a present for you."

I was touched but also confused. How could the Chinaman have anything for me?

"Close your eyes tight for one moment."

He was not usually bossy.

"You may now open them." And when I did, I got a big shock. Of course he was there, but also Mama, the old Danny, and Frank.

The three of them were smiling at me, but they were silent. Slowly, as I let the quiet take over, I began to hear the music that their bodies were swaying to. It was the nameless ritualized dance with ancient movements that Kwai Chang and I had practiced over and over. It always was serious when he and I did it. Now it was completely different, and I felt a deep bubble of laughter from the middle part of my stomach.

Frank the clerk was on the end. And he was a joy to see, his shirt flung open and the muscles at his waist moving and contracting with effort. His black skin was no longer gray, and I thought that if I moved closer I would be able to touch him and smell his scent, the deep musty scent of love and desire.

Mama and the old Danny were the uncoordinated ones with their interpretation of kung fu. I nearly fell on the floor from laughter when Danny tried to raise his leg but couldn't bring it high because of the fat that encircled his waist. But now there was a change that I saw with my heart. It was glorious fat,

fat that floated, fat that made me love him and feel his joy of life. And I was happy to see his giant body moving with grace.

And then there was Mama, only her eyes were focused and concentrated on moving as precisely as Frank was moving. Her thighs were free, covered with material that moved as gently as she did. It was almost serious until Mama's wig fell on the floor, and she forgot everything she'd learned about grace and noise when she plopped down to pick it up.

"Oh, God, I done caught a cramp in my leg." It was the old Danny again, hopping on one leg, making moaning sounds and laughing at himself at the same time. They all collapsed in a heap, and there was laughter that moved from them to me and tickled my heart.

Kwai Chang was smiling widely now, something he had never done before, and shaking his head as he began to disappear. And so did they, little by little. I was left with the knowledge that they were where they were and I was getting ready to graduate high school and go to college.

We are all moving, searching in this life for some happiness. Some never find it at all. But I was wrong in believing that it was only Kwai Chang and me doing the searching. Everyone searches. The real challenge is in the finding and the keeping.

TWENTY-SEVEN

WE WERE CURSED DAUGHTERS. THERESA SHRUGGED WHEN I told her this and said that maybe I should stop smoking so much pot or try not smoking and reading at the same time because it had too much of an effect on my imagination.

Her tone was light, but her eyes were dead in the middle, and I knew that she felt the same as I did about being cursed.

"Pam, things are bad. Real bad. But I know they gonna get better. They can't get no worse. They just can't."

I was close to her, close enough to smell her unwashed body and dirty hair. Sweat and Dixie Peach. Fear too. And like Kwai Chang taught, I let go. The rigid place in the small of my back, the tightness in the middle of my stomach—I let it all out with a breath and reached for my sister, putting my arms around her tightly and holding on. And she hugged me back with all her might.

"Ain't nuthin' else bad gonna happen to us. You'll see. Mama and Daddy gone is enough. God ain't mean, He ain't like that. He gonna make sure nuthin' else bad happen." And I held her tighter because finally she was crying and so was I.

But Theresa was wrong. Something else bad happened.

MONIQUE'S HEAD WAS BOWED OVER PURE JOY, SO AT FIRST I thought she was cooing to the baby or kissing her hand, something we all did. I was in the kitchen. The only sound was the hum of the refrigerator. I was making a peanut butter and jelly sandwich with lots of peanut butter and only a swish of jelly. I had a cold glass of milk on the counter and an apple peeled and cored. I couldn't help but think I was eating like this because of Danny. He made me want to eat good food, made me want to give this a try instead of stuffing myself on Ring Dings or Yo-dels. And that was funny considering he had been one of the biggest people I'd ever known. But then I figured that he got his bigness from eating good food like collard greens and mashed potatoes, not from junk.

She stood without speaking until I finished making my sandwich and glanced over at her.

"I can't stay here."

There was no pretending that I didn't know what she was talking about. I put the knife down and picked up the top of the peanut butter jar, getting it ready to go back in the fridge. Normally people don't put peanut butter there, but we did. Too many roaches to leave stuff out. Almost everything was in there—the bread, the mustard, and even the fruit Danny brought over.

"Every time I look at y'all, every time Nona touch me, I see your mama. I brought this pain to y'all and I can't take it back. I can't live with it neither."

The baby squirmed and reached small fingers to Monique's hoop earrings. Her mother caught her before she could do any damage and pressed the hand to her lips in the same worshipful manner we all used with Pure Joy.

"I'm gonna leave the baby here. I ain't got no place to stay yet."

"This will kill Nona."

"I already done that."

She moved closer and handed the baby to me, almost tossing her into my arms. She turned quickly, and I understood that she could not face us anymore, not me or the baby. She knew how wrong this was, she knew how much more she was getting ready to heap on our family.

"Y'all gonna be all right. I'm giving you this here baby to keep. Love her like she your baby, okay?"

But she was not crying and there was no tremor in her voice to make me believe that she cared at all. I hefted Joy to my shoulder and touched her face with mine. I went to the kitchen doorway.

The baby put her mouth to my cheek and slobbered. I laughed despite the sadness in my chest that now felt like a large unmoving lump. There was no relief from this burden except when I held Joy.

THERESA CRIED. SHE SHOOK MY HAND OFF HER SHOULDER AND reached for Joy and kept crying.

"How we gonna tell Nona? Who gonna tell her? Oh, Jesus. She gonna break."

But it seemed to me that Theresa was breaking. She kept asking questions and rocking the baby, who looked like she was scared with all the rocking and crying going on.

"Give me the baby. You ain't holding her right."

My sister stopped long enough to hand me the baby and sat on the sofa, almost shuddering.

"Look, at least she ain't take the baby. Nona'll get over her. Somebody else will be along."

Theresa took a deep breath and waited. I knew what she was doing. She was counting until she could get it together. I waited.

"Who gonna tell Nona?" Theresa asked.

"I think I'll have to. She ain't gonna want to hear it from you or Danny." I was surprised at myself for volunteering and even more surprised when Theresa nodded as though what I said made sense.

NONA CAME THROUGH THE DOOR AT SIX-THIRTY. SHE'D stopped to play some hoops in the park.

"Hey, where my two babies? Mama home."

She was loud and playful, and sometimes she said, "Daddy's home," but we stopped her from that by telling her that P.J. might get confused.

"Just because you a dyke and like women don't mean you gotta act like a man." Danny said this, and we waited for Nona to puff up or talk mean to him because he was trying to tell her what to do. But she listened and nodded as if he was saying some wise things. Damn if we didn't know how she would react half the time.

Theresa and Danny had left sometime earlier. We all thought it would be best if I had some privacy with Nona. They hadn't taken the baby, though, and I was wrestling with her and smiling at her when Nona walked in. It was something to see how Pure Joy's head snapped around when she heard Nona's voice and how she tried to get out of my arms to my sister. Nona smiled and walked up to me, taking the baby, holding her tight against her sweaty body.

"Where Monique?"

I was not skilled at this. Tears had already started to form at the corners of my eyes.

"I gotta talk to you about that."

Nona paused in holding Pure Joy up above her head. There was knowledge already in her eyes. She sat down on the sofa next to me, letting the baby walk up her stomach and onto her chest, over and over again.

"What you got to tell me, sis?"

"Monique done gone. She left you, us. She say she can't live with the guilt no more. She think she helped kill Mama."

"Look at you, girl, you can walk. Can't you, girl? You just the smartest thing. Yes you are. I think you even gonna be smarter than your aunt Pam and she about the smartest one in this house."

Nona kept playing with the baby until finally she gave up trying to hold on to her feelings and scooped her close in her arms.

"She gonna take our baby?"

"She told me that she gonna leave her with us. That she ain't got no place right now."

"That mean she gonna be back to get her."

"Maybe. I don't know."

"What you think we should do?"

Nona was staring at me with frightened eyes.

"We gonna keep our baby for as long as we can. If she come back, we gonna have to give her up. Pure Joy ain't no kin—no blood kin, that is. But we ain't movin' no more. Her mama got the right to see her if she want."

"But Pam, she ain't no kinda mama. How she gonna just up and leave her baby? Our mama ain't never left us. She was crazy but she still love us enough to stay."

Nona's voice sounded like tears, but nothing came down her face. She put her head to Pure Joy's stomach and made raspberry sounds so that the baby giggled and put her hands on the top of Nona's head.

"Nona, I can't say nuthin' about Monique. I don't know enough about her to say nuthin'. But I do know that sometimes people feel they gotta go. And that's what she did."

"This hurts. Hurts so bad I can't hardly breathe. I never thought I'd feel like this again. When Daddy left I hurt like this, when Mama died. I didn't think nobody else would leave. I thought we was set now."

She surprised me. I didn't think she had cared when Daddy left.

She sat with me for a few more minutes and then gave the baby back to me.

"I'm gonna shower and lay down for a little while. I gotta think about this. You all right with Miss Thing?"

"I'm fine."

Nona leaned forward and kissed me on the cheek. Her face was closer to mine than it had ever been, and she stared into my eyes.

"I'm glad you ain't never gonna leave. I'm glad you my sister."

She turned and left before I could think of anything to say. Pure Joy was fussing, ready for a bottle, and I heard the water from the shower and thought that Nona could weep alone in peace, her salty tears washed away to the same place as the sweat that coated her thin body.

"Girl, I'ma get you your bottle. Stop trying to bite my titty."

TWENTY-EIGHT

ON THE FIRST DAY OF COLLEGE I WAS SCARED. I'D BEEN TO THE campus once with Theresa. But it was different when I was alone. People around me were throwing Frisbees on the lawn and laughing together in small groups of two or three. This was no different from high school, the cliques that wandered the hallways, the giggly girls and Earth Shoe–wearing white kids. But I felt blacker than I ever had. Black as in my hair was different and so were my lips and my clothes.

I took a back seat in my freshman composition class and kept my head down, studying shoes, the floor, anything to keep from making eye contact with anyone. I was cursing inside, telling myself that I didn't belong, and cursing Theresa for making me, and cursing the guidance counselor for whatever he did to get me in this place where I wasn't comfortable. And then I heard the voice and I had to look up.

She was taller than me, probably a good five inches or so, and she held her body erect. Dressed in red, she had positioned herself near the chalkboard and written her name on it with a sprawling script. People were quiet when she started talking, and there was an excitement in the air—maybe because it was the first day, maybe because they were already taken with this woman in front of us. She traveled away from the podium and smiled with white teeth and lips that were friendly. She met the eyes of all who would meet hers. I was too shy.

"I expect you to take your seats so we can begin learning. My name is Lydia St. Martin, and I'm going to teach you all that you need to know about freshman composition this year. And it's important for you to know that I take learning seriously, teaching seriously, and each one of you seriously."

I held my breath. She was black as the night, and suddenly I felt relief and gratitude that I had finally arrived and there was someone of my colored flesh in front of me. And I stared at her skin—that being the only common thing between us that I knew of besides her pussy—and realized that if she could be in front of us teaching, then I had the ability to do it too.

College I will do, I said to myself. *I have the dreams and hopes of the three that left me and the four that are at my side.* When her eyes traveled the room again, I met them and I nodded. And I imagined I saw a slight nod and a smile in return. I was ready for whatever would come next.

EPILOGUE

I GOT A JOB WAITING TABLES, BUT I LOOKED ALL THE TIME. I hoped that one day he might come to me. That he would stand in his carpenter's overalls and smile down at me shyly when I returned the love that he had never been able to give me when he lived with us.

One day a coppery-skinned black man sat at my table. The hair at his temples was gray and his speech precise, the way educated island men speak.

He gave the menu back. His hands attracted me, blunt callused fingers with jagged nails, split across the top, ashy knuckles, and wrinkles spread across the back haphazardly, veined and strong. I breathed deeply near his chair, the scent of wood and metal shavings filling my nose. We became lovers.

"DO YOU MIND THAT I AM SO MUCH OLDER THAN YOU?" HE WAS serious. We were in bed, my face buried in his chest, near the baby fine hairs surrounding his nipples.

"No."

We both sighed in the darkness. I listened to his heartbeat, *da-thump, da-thump, da-thump.* I licked his fingers one by one, my tongue softening the cuticles around his dented nails.

"Do you mind that I have a wife and children and that I won't leave them?"

"Tell me about your children, your sons."

"Ah, they are handsome, men already."

Listening to his crisp, lilting Jamaican accent as he recited first the litany against his wife and then the virtues of his sons, I was sated.

"I have stayed because of them. I could not leave my sons to be raised by a woman. They need to know how to be men—to stay even when they want to go." Tears sat like little rivers in my eyes, but I would not let him see me cry. I buried my face in his wide shoulders and kissed his sweet, thick neck.

Later I sat on his lap and made him laugh and forget about the gap-toothed, mealy-mouthed woman waiting for him. At the door he bowed like a courtly gentleman and kissed my hand. When it closed I stood on my toes to watch him through the peephole. At the elevator he glanced back and smiled. I wondered if he nailed rugs or shaped wood into smooth-edged door frames at home.

Then I thought of Kwai Chang Caine and sighed. I saw him in my mind's eye, shouldering his pack and putting a tattered brown hat on his head, his stringy hair gently moving as he did. He nodded in my direction. There were no parting words between us, as there had never been between my father and I. But this time I knew. And it was all right for now.

ABOUT THE AUTHOR

BONNIE J. GLOVER was born in Florence, Alabama, but grew up in the mean streets of Brooklyn's East New York, where *The Middle Sister* is set. She attended Rafael Cordero Junior High School and John Dewey High School, both in Brooklyn. She obtained a B.S. at Florida Agricultural and Mechanical University's School of Business and Industry in Tallahassee, Florida, and eventually a law degree from Stetson University College of Law in St. Petersburg, Florida. She currently works for the Department of Veterans Affairs, Office of Regional Counsel. She lives in Pembroke Pines, Florida, with her husband, Craig, and two sons, Matt and Ben.